A Rose by Any Other Name

ROBERT F. BOLLENDORF

authorHOUSE®

AuthorHouse™
1663 Liberty Drive
Bloomington, IN 47403
www.authorhouse.com
Phone: 1 (800) 839-8640

This is a work of fiction. All of the characters, names, incidents, organizations, and dialogue
in this novel are either the products of the author's imagination or are used fictitiously.

Published by AuthorHouse 10/06/2017

ISBN: 978-1-5462-1035-1 (sc)
ISBN: 978-1-5462-1034-4 (e)

Print information available on the last page.

This book is printed on acid-free paper.

Because of the dynamic nature of the Internet, any web addresses or links contained in
this book may have changed since publication and may no longer be valid. The views
expressed in this work are solely those of the author and do not necessarily reflect the
views of the publisher, and the publisher hereby disclaims any responsibility for them.

DEDICATION

In the 40 years I taught at College of DuPage, I had the privilege of teaching many wonderful students who have gone on to work with abused women at DuPage Family Shelter; dozens more have worked in addiction treatment centers, mental health and corrections facilities. This book is dedicated to all of you. Thanks for all the lives you have saved and the people you have become. I learned so much from you.

CHAPTER 1

The face in the picture still looked beautiful even after fading two weeks in the August sun and wrinkling in the recent rains. The weathered photo now just barely clung to the tree, not unlike the hope most had of finding her alive.

Another storm was kicking upstream in the western sky, a common occurrence as the seasons transitioned from summer to fall. Thunderheads began climbing to the heavens, hurrying dusk along in the late afternoon heat. Flashes of lightning streaked across the dense darkness and lit up the tiny town of Keshena, Wisconsin, just as the bright sun had done earlier in the day, if only momentarily.

The first streak illuminated the picture one more time; the next lit up the bare tree as the picture rode the wind into the stand of trees alongside the Wolf River that ran through the middle of town.

Lucy Teller was passing by in her patrol car just as the picture tore loose. She decided to get out and look for it before it ended up in the river and worked its way to Shawano Lake or even Lake Winnebago, 100 miles to the south. In the two weeks since Rose Waukau had gone missing, the only luck Lucy had finding the young woman was bad luck.

She thought of the girl in the photo as she tromped through the underbrush with her flashlight shining on the ground. Rose had worked so hard. She made the honor roll all through grade school and high school, then went onto college on an academic and music scholarships, where she excelled in playing the alto clarinet in the band.

Her hard work seemed to be paying off. She earned good grades at St.

Norman's College her freshman year and easily made friends in the band. She was even dating the St. Norman's quarterback, who had dreams of going pro.

But part of the mystery that kept Lucy awake at night was that much of that seemed to change by the end of spring semester. While her grades were still acceptable, they had sharply declined. Her friends reported her "drifting away." She had broken up with her boyfriend, and he was confused about what had happened between them.

Grasping the windswept paper, Lucy so wished the photo of the girl with brown eyes, black hair and high cheekbones was real. She folded it up and tucked it in her vest pocket. She knew if she hung it back up, it would only be blown off again by the storm. Besides, the people from the community who went by it every day didn't need a reminder of the pain they felt since Rose's disappearance.

Rose Waukau was a shining example of all the progress that the Menominees had been making in their schools and their community. She was in one of the first groups of seniors with a 90% graduation rate. She was a point guard on the girls' basketball team that had made it all the way to state, and was an active member of the choir.

After graduation, Rose had stayed in Keshena and worked at the new Subway until the middle of August. She was excited to leave for school, but found it hard to leave the safety of her family and the Rez, even though they were only an hour's drive away. Like many Indian reservations, hers had its share of problems, but it was still home and where she grew up. Most of her friends were staying home and attending the College of Menominee Nation, a new school that was already making a significant impact in the community. Tuition at St. Norman's was out of the question for most of her friends, as it would have been for Rose, if she hadn't received her scholarships.

Though classes were still several weeks off, Rose had gone early to begin band practice in anticipation of the halftime show during the first home football games. Rose walked off the football field with her new friends, sweat running down the side of her cheek and moisture dotting her t-shirt, but still looking beautiful in the midday sun. She had quickly bonded with many of the other band members, and they did a lot to ease her homesickness.

While they were talking and laughing, she caught the eye Colt Dickson, the junior quarterback who had been starting for the Dragons since his freshman year. Colt asked some of his teammates who she was, but none of them knew. Several phone calls later, he tracked her down through a fellow bandmate, who begrudgingly gave him Rose's name and dorm number, disappointed it wasn't her who Colt was interested in.

The next day a florist delivered a single red rose to her dorm room with a note that read: *"This rose is pretty, but make sure you don't stand too close to it, or it will wilt in shame." – Colt Dickson*

CHAPTER 2

Bobbie Brandt rode her bike along the Fox River in Green Bay, enjoying one of the last days near 80 degrees and one of her last days of freedom before starting her new job. On Monday, she would start as a counselor at St. Norman's. After taking some time off following her brother's murder, she had returned to school to finish her bachelor's degree, and then went on to get her master's in counseling. She specialized in counseling women and had done an internship at a woman's shelter.

Tom, her boyfriend of several years, had found someone else while Bobbie was away trying to find a direction in her life. She was devastated at first, but learned to stand on her own and soon began to think she would likely live a single life.

But when she returned to school, she met Austin. He was kind and gentle and she fell in love with him while they completed a community service project in a preschool situated in a particularly poor area of Green Bay. As she watched him interact with the children, she saw his kind and gentle nature come through. It was something he hid from his peers and teachers.

After a few months of dating, the topic of marriage came up, but there was a hitch: Austin was in ROTC and had planned to enlist in the Marines before he met Bobbie. Now that he was serving in Afghanistan, Bobbie decided to sign up as a proctor in the women's dorm. Surely that would help eat up some of the agonizing free time that she spent thinking of Austin and missing him. She had considered getting her doctorate

4

in counseling, and believed that if she lived in a dorm, she'd have more opportunity to study and be closer to her classes.

Back on the blacktop trail, she watched the river and studied the people she passed on the trail before noticing a girl in front of her biking at nearly the same speed. Bobbie was working at being a little more outgoing and decided to speed up to see if the girl might like some company.

When she managed to pull up next to her, she commented on what a great day it was for a bike ride. The girl had obviously been lost in thought and was startled by Bobbie's comment. She appeared to be noticing her surrounding for the first time and she replied, "I guess so. I'm afraid my mind was back home in Indiana and I wasn't paying much attention."

"I was looking for some company, but I'll let you get back to Indiana," Bobbie laughed.

"Oh, no, please," the girl answered sincerely, "I need to be here and enjoy my time now. I'd love some company."

Bobbie soon learned that not only was Ada a freshman at St. Norman's, she was also living in the same dorm where she would be living. Most dorms no longer had curfew hours for girls, nor did they keep them from bringing boys to their rooms, but the St. Norman's administration had decided to experiment. They now had one dorm for girls that had both a curfew and advisors on each floor, not just for supervision, but to provide a resource for the girls in helping them deal with roommate conflicts and other problems that might arise in being away from home for the first time.

During the ride, they decided to take the trail until the blacktop ended outside Manitowoc, about 40 miles round trip. Ada talked a lot on the trip. While she listened, Bobbie tried utilizing the skills she learned in her counseling courses. It was so fun to bring to consciousness her first impressions of people and then see if they were verified as the relationship continued. She had guessed that Ada was normally a lot quieter, but the nervousness of being on her own for the first time and starting the new experience of college and meeting the first person she could talk to had brought the flood of words. That was quickly followed by the thought that maybe Ada was trying on some new behaviors around new people. Despite Ada's beauty, Bobbie thought she picked up a lack of esteem and was surprised that someone as pretty and personable as Ada would lack self worth.

Bobbie smiled when she realized while she had gotten so caught up in her impressions, she had failed to pay attention to all that Ada was saying.

"I think you're going to be good at this counseling stuff," Ada said. "I usually don't talk this much, but I've decided to try being more outgoing now that I'm on my own."

Bingo! Bobbie thought. Sigmund Freud, you've got nothing on me!

With their shared love of biking, they set a date for the following weekend to do the Fox River trail again.

CHAPTER 3

The next day had turned cold, which made it easier for Bobbie to settle into work and begin arranging her office. She paused from her task to stare at the Fox River flowing outside her window. She wondered what the year would bring, and her thoughts soon turned to Austin and how he was handling life in Afghanistan.

Carefully, she pulled a picture out of the box of personal items she had brought to decorate her efficiency apartment at the dorm and her office. There was Austin smiling at her, but it was the rifle he held and the camouflage outfit he wore that sent chills down her back. His letters spoke mostly of his work building schools and meeting the young students who would benefit from his efforts. He seemed particularly pleased that he was helping provide young girls the opportunity to attend school for the first time.

But it was this satisfaction that scared Bobbie the most, as it made him a target for the hatred of the Taliban. Her mind soon turned to the brave young girl who had become a strong advocate for educating girls after being shot in the face by the Taliban for attending school.

A knock interrupted her thoughts, and Bobbie stood to see Ada and another young woman in her doorway. "Ada, I'm so glad you're my first visitor," she said, and extended her hand to the second woman.

"Hi, I'm Bobbie Brandt." The words had flowed naturally, just as she had begun to wonder how she should introduce herself to students.

"I'm Caroline," she replied. "Just want you to know I don't need your help. I'm only here because my new roomy said you were nice, and that you might not be too hard on me when I come in drunk."

Ada and Caroline contrasted each other in every way. Ada was tall and toned, no doubt from her years of volleyball that had earned her a scholarship. She was from Carmen, Indiana, the product of parents originally from Virginia who protected and doted on their only child. She had a Southern charm with just a hint of a drawl. Her face was soft and kind, with light brown hair that belied a dark complexion – the result of a summer job lifeguarding at the pool.

Caroline was short, and though she was attractive, she did little to highlight her features. Her sweatshirt – a few sizes too big – hung lifelessly on her and reached to the middle of her thighs. Though she had a pretty face, she seemed to wear an expression that dared you to approach her: *Start a conversation at your own risk.*

She came to college from a group home in Milwaukee, the last in a long line of residences that had started when her parents were killed in a car accident. Her father had been a college professor and her mother a pharmacist before they died. Despite being a brilliant young woman, she was never able to get over the bitterness about the life she could have had, nor could she express any gratitude for the intelligence her parents had passed along to her.

Bobbie and Caroline stared for a moment, sizing each other up: Bobbie looking for ways she could connect with Caroline, and Caroline looking for ways she could protect herself from another do-gooder.

"So would you like to join Ada and me on our ride next weekend?" Bobbie asked.

"Well, weather permitting, I'll find a good book and join you at the start. The I'll wave goodbye and read til you come back," she said. "Maybe I'll find a book that mentions exercise and skim it. I don't suppose you'd buy a six-pack for me to drink while I wait for you?" Caroline asked, fully knowing the answer.

"I don't think that fits my job description very well," Bobbie replied with a smile.

CHAPTER 4

On the St. Norman's football field, Colt Dickson threw a pass toward Eli Bolt, but underthrew it again. These were two guys who were used to connecting on nearly every play in practice and had run the play countless times and rarely missed. On the next play, Colt counted on Eli's twin brother, Ethan, to cut right, but he instead cut left and another pass hit the dry dirt, leaving a cloud of dust.

Colt looked disgusted, and as usual, when things went wrong, he blamed someone else. He pointed the other way to Ethan, who, being accustomed to taking the blame for Colt's mistakes, just shrugged his shoulders.

After practice, Colt, the Bolt twins and his other two roommates were resting in their townhouse on the edge of campus between the brutal double-day football practices. It was a much nicer place than the living expenses of their scholarships would allow, but Colt's dad was rich and paid the difference.

Colt lived in the house with his brother, Danny, who was a paraplegic, so the townhouse was set up for wheelchair access. His friend, Matt, a hockey player, and two of his teammates from the football team also lived there. Eli and Ethan Bolt were a big reason why both the Green Dragons and Colt were as successful as they were. Both were pass catchers and Colt's favorite targets.

The Bolts, fraternal twins from the Chicago suburbs, looked like surfer dudes from California with light blond hair and deep tans. Eli was taller than Ethan and fast as lightning. After high school, Big Ten schools recruited him, but he refused to play without his brother. Ethan was a quarterback but converted to receiver in college. He was a little shorter and slower than his brother, but he had great hands and was a terrific route runner. He also was good at making extra yards after he caught the ball. He turned out to be a possession receiver – a lot like Tom Waddle of the Chicago Bears – and though Colt may have thought he could be great without them, outside observers thought otherwise.

The three of them, along with their star running back Corey Ruger, had all started their freshman year, and by this point, had developed a strong bond between them so that Colt could throw a pass and know – without looking – where the brothers would be on the field. Often teams would load up on defensive backs to try and stop them. Colt would then hand off to Corey, who would leave a trail of the smaller d-backs behind him. Many of those smaller, speedy guys ended up wishing they had stuck to track in college after being hit by Corey.

The exhaustion of the workout had each of them too tired to speak or even think much. Matt and Danny had just gotten back from working out at the gym and were nearly as tired. Though Danny couldn't walk, he had a strong upper body and often entered racing and weightlifting competitions for the physically challenged. Matt was already preparing for hockey season. Even when they weren't exhausted, most of their conversations were about whatever sporting event they were watching on TV.

CHAPTER 5

The next day, the sun and warmer weather returned to the area, and with classes not yet started, Ada decided to sit in the stands and watch cheerleading tryouts. She tucked her hair up underneath a baseball cap, and her brown skin glistened in the warm sun.

As she caught Colt's eye, he missed a handoff to Corey and got the ire of his coach.

"Dickson, you still on summer break?" he asked sarcastically. "You haven't had your head on straight since you got back here."

"Sorry, coach," he said. "Thought I saw a ghost," he mumbled under his breath.

"Our season starts in two weeks, and if we're still playing like this, don't expect to win a single game!" the coach yelled at the group.

Something about seeing Ada seemed to wake him up, and the rest of the practice went much better.

Though cheerleading tryouts had long ended, Ada still sat quietly in the sun watching the football practice, though her mind drifted back home. Colt's voice broke the silence.

"I can't decide if you look like someone I know or if we've met somewhere before," he lied, knowing exactly where he had seen her. "My name's Colt. What's yours?"

"Ada," she replied, still a bit dazed at having been ripped from thoughts of her home, back to the reality of Green Bay.

"We get a lot of people at our games, but not too many at practice, especially before school starts," he said. "Here to see someone in particular?"

"Actually, yes," Ada replied. "I was here to encourage my friend during cheerleading tryouts, but when that ended, I thought I'd stay and soak up some sun and see what kind of football team I could expect to see. Looks like they're still a little rusty, but they'll get better."

"Are you a student here?" Colt asked. "If so, you must be new, because there's no way you could be walking around here for a year or more and me not notice you," he replied, without waiting for Ada's response.

She blushed from the implication. "I'm a freshman. I'm in the Lombardi dorm," she replied.

"Isn't that the one with the stricter rules?" he asked.

"Yes," she replied. "My parents thought I should concentrate on studies and volleyball my first year."

"Well, I can understand that. If I was your old man, I'd have you under lock and key," Colt grinned. "So…you're a volleyball player, eh?"

Ada nodded.

"How about I pick you up tomorrow after football practice and show you around the area.? I can help you get acclimated before classes start," said Colt.

"That would be nice," Ada replied. "I'd like that."

"Don't eat dinner," he said. "I'm always starved after practice and we'll grab a bite to eat."

CHAPTER 6

Colt showed up at Ada and Caroline's room at 6 the following evening. Ada was still in the bathroom that was shared with the room next to theirs, so Caroline answered the soft knock. She opened the door and eyed him from head to toe. "I expected you to be taller," she remarked.

Caroline loved catching people off guard, especially men, and especially a man full of himself. She could tell immediately this one was one of them.

"You must be Ada's roommate," he replied. "Seems like it could be a long year for her."

"That depends on how much time she spends with you."

"Let's start over," Colt replied, turning on his Texas charm. "Hi, my name's Colt. I'm here to pick up Ada. You must be her roommate. What did you say your name was?"

"I didn't say," Caroline sneered. "But I'll check to see if she's ready."

"Ada!" she yelled. "Prince Charming is here."

Caroline turned back toward the doorway.

"She'll be here in a sec," she replied. "Oh, and sorry, but no men allowed in the room." Then she closed the door quietly in his face.

Ada walked out a few seconds later, smiling. "I guess you met Caroline."

"Oh, you mean Madam de Vil?" he snickered.

"Actually, we get along great," Ada replied. "I think she was mad cuz she had to go to dinner alone. We have a couple other friends, but one had a cheerleader meeting and another an R.A. meeting."

Ada was expecting dinner at a simple fast food joint, but instead, Colt took her to Lombardi's Steakhouse in Green Bay.

"Can't live in this area without knowing something about the history of the Packers," he told her, before filling her in on Curly Lambeau and the early Packers.

"If you're interested, I can take you on a whole tour of this town and show you where the Packers first played, Vince Lombardi's house, the Packer Hall of Fame – you can even run out the tunnel onto Lambeau Field!" Colt said with excitement pulsing through his voice.

While this might have been boring to a lot of people, Ada was intrigued. Despite being from Indiana, Ada and her parents were Packer fans. It all started when her dad went to a football camp in Florida run by Bart Starr. Her dad had found the man so genuine and caring and, at the time, there was no professional team in the Carolinas, so he started following the Packers just at the time they were beginning to improve for the first time since the Lombardi era in the 60s. Colt grew up a Dallas Cowboys fan, but since moving to Green Bay, Packer scouts had been by to see him play.

Ada had grown up wearing Packer pajamas long before she began watching games with her folks. At first, it was just the fun of having snacks in the TV room and sitting on the couch with her parents. They weren't big TV watchers, so the chance to sit between her mom and dad uninterrupted for three hours was a real treat. She soon started to understand the game and was caught up in the excitement as much as they were. When she started playing sports herself, she saw the same excitement in her parents' faces as they cheered for her and her teammates.

Colt and Ada sat talking for two hours. The restaurant wasn't busy on a weeknight, so no one was waiting for their table. The waitress had seen Colt before, so she knew a big tip would follow if the service was good, and she gave them their space.

At first, he touched her arm ever so briefly when making a point, but as the evening progressed, his hand lingered there longer. Ada noticed the touch right away and looked forward to the next one. She had dated in high school. but as she thought about it now, those were boys and this was a man. Now, she was a girl, but feeling more like a woman. She felt his touch at the source as the electricity moved up her arm.

CHAPTER 7

Back at home in Keshena, Lucy Teller reviewed her notes on the Rose Waukau case. She had disappeared on August 3rd while home on summer break from St. Norman's. She finished her shift at the Subway at 8 pm, then told her co-workers she was tired and not interested in going with them to watch the volleyball games at the War Bonnet. The War Bonnet was a bar in town that once had a reputation for patrons that liked to fight after a few drinks, but new owners had taken it over and black listed those patrons known to cause trouble. They also fixed it up added a gift shop and volleyball courts and put greater emphasis on the food they served. As a result there was an increase in business for Whites and Indians alike.

She left the parking lot that the restaurant shared with a Save-a-Lot grocery store and a Family Dollar about 8:10, and was seen by a couple of people heading toward home. Several people outside the War Bonnet said they saw her drive by around 8:15 when she beeped and waved. They described her as smiling and showing no indication of distress.

She would have crossed the bridge over the Wolf River onto Highway 47, her house was just off the that road at the end of a long driveway. She stopped to check in with some neighbors who promised her parents to look after her while they took her younger brothers and sister on a fishing trip before they had to go back to school.

Lucy interviewed the neighbors, who said Rose hung around for about a half hour, then decided to head home to watch TV and go to bed. They remarked that she seemed tired after a day of work, but not any more upset than she had been all summer.

They said she had seemed somewhat depressed over the summer after breaking up with her boyfriend just before school had let out, but told them several times that she thought she was better off without him. She had decided to take a break from any serious relationships for a while, and was just anxious to get back to school and her extracurricular activities.

By the time she left, it was completely dark, and though they couldn't see her house about a quarter mile away due to the thick wooded area, they had not heard any unusual sounds, screams or gunshots coming from that direction. Traffic on 47 was the usual. It was difficult for Lucy to interview the parents who came right home when Rose didn't report for work the next day. When they arrived home, Rose's bed had not been slept in, but other than that, there was nothing unusual about how the house looked. There were no fingerprints belonging to anyone other than family or people who had visited the home as invited guests. They had called Rose between 9 and 9:30 and there was no answer, but they assumed she was watching volleyball at the War Bonnet. Her cell phone had gone right to voicemail.

In an earlier conversation, Rose said she really missed them and wished she had just forgotten about making a few extra bucks over the summer and gone with them. Her mother thought maybe Rose's voice had cracked just a little when she spoke. Recalling that conversation, her mother started to cry, and through her tears said, "I wished I would have asked her again if she was alright."

Lucy talked to Rose's father, Jim Waukau. "Is there any chance that Rose decided at the last minute to visit a friend?" she asked.

"If she did, it would be totally out of character for her, especially not letting us know," he replied. "We've never had to put restrictions on Rose; she knew what we expected and always did it. But, she's at the age where she might decide it's time to cut the apron strings, or just do something out of character to see how it feels," he continued. "I watch the news and work at the tribal clinic. I see and talk to parents every day who say 'my kid would never do that,' only to find out their kid did do that. No one would be happier than I to find out she did something out of the ordinary and is safe somewhere, but I doubt it."

"I've learned that her former boyfriend went back to school yesterday," said Lucy. "Any chance she had a change of heart and decided to go see him?"

"I wish I knew more about that relationship," Jim said. "She was very closed-mouth about it and I think he wanted it that way."

"Why do you say that?" Lucy asked.

"Well there were a few times during the year that she would be on the phone with us and he would show up. She would immediately say, 'gotta go' and quickly hung up," he said.

"Any idea why that was the case?" asked Lucy.

"No. I asked her about it once and she said I was imagining things, but I don't believe I was," Jim said.

"Did Rose date much in high school?" Lucy asked.

"A little bit, but no one very seriously," he answered.

"Was there anyone – male or female – who might have been jealous of the path she seemed to be following?" Lucy asked.

"What do you mean, 'path'?" Jim asked.

"I mean she left the Rez," said Lucy. "She attended a private school. Maybe someone felt that she was turning her nose up at the people she grew up with."

"Rose wasn't like that," Jim answered defensively. "Even in high school, where there was certainly some of that between various groups, Rose was friendly to everyone. I heard that numerous times from teachers at conferences, and her close friends would even tease her about it."

"That's partly what I mean," Rose shot back quickly. "Everyone I talk to says how friendly and nice she was. That makes some people a little nauseous. She seemed to have everything – grades, music, sports, friends, incredible looks, loving parents, and she was humble about it to boot."

"I suppose there could have been people who felt that way," Jim answered. "You read about these kids who walk into schools and kill people, and no one seems to have any warning about it. But I didn't know anyone who felt that way. Maybe I better warn her siblings," Jim said, tearing up. "They idolize her. Maybe they need to make more mistakes."

"I know," Lucy said, fighting back a tear of her own. "Having kids myself, it seems even when you're doing right, something is wrong."

"If you think of anything or hear anything, no matter how trivial it may seem, call me," Lucy said, handing him a card.

Lucy then interviewed Rose's closest friends, asking the same questions and unfortunately getting the same answers. In passing, they mentioned a kid named Billy West who would frequently tease Rose about being Miss Goody Two Shoes, or Miss Perfect, and since Billy seemed to have a number of problems at school and home, he could easily have been jealous of Rose.

Lucy was already familiar with the Wests, having gone there more than once on domestic violence calls. They lived right down the road from her on Rabbit Ridge Road. On her way home, she decided to stop. They lived in a trailer, and Lucy pulled into the long driveway and stopped about halfway up and waited to see someone in the window before getting out of her squad.

As she started up the driveway, she was startled by a barking and growling dog she had awoken from its nap. Just when she was sure she'd soon be on her way to the ER with a dog stuck to her leg, the dog jerked backwards and yelped as his chain reached its full length. Undeterred, the dog tried again to break free, but this time, more aware of his boundary, rose up on his hind legs and bared the teeth he was hoping to sink into Lucy's leg.

Finally, the door to the trailer opened and a strong voice yelled, "Buck! Hush!"

The dog obeyed and went back to his nap.

"I've been waiting for you, Officer Teller," Billy said. "What took you so long?"

Lucy Looked at Billy quizzically. "What do you mean?"

"Well, Rose has been missing a while now, I thought you'd be over much sooner to slap the cuffs on me."

"Do you have a guilty conscience, Billy?" Lucy asked.

"Of course not, I'm a psychopath," he sneered. "Don't the shrinks say I don't have a conscience?"

"I don't know about that, but I am impressed that you know something about psychological diagnosis," Lucy replied.

"Believe it or not, there are times in school when I actually pay attention," Billy replied. "I liked my intro to psych class."

"Well, since you brought it up, what do you know about Rose's disappearance?" Lucy asked.

"Just what I've learned from hanging around," he replied. "That she left work at night and the next day she didn't show up. And…just to anticipate your next question…I liked Rose and I think she liked me," he said. "In spite of us traveling in different circles, and the fact that I was always on her case, she'd just smile at me and say, 'Oh, Billy when are you going to stop hiding behind that tough exterior of yours and show us the teddy bear you really are?' I would've asked her out, but I didn't want to put her in a position she couldn't get out of. I thought I was lucky to have what I did with her and didn't want to screw that up."

"Must have been frustrating to know you could only get so far with her," Lucy responded.

"I'm a poor Indian," he said. "I know all about living with limits and frustration."

"I guess you do," she said. "Well, if in the process of hanging out, you learn anything that might help me find Lucy, let me know."

"You can count on that, officer," Billy said, looking her right in the eyes.

"Usually I would think that was so much bullshit, but I believe you would, Billy West," Lucy said. "I think I just saw the teddy bear."

With that comment, Lucy saw him smile for the first time.

On the way home, she thought of the moment she just encountered. Her husband Ray was always telling her we have to stay in the moment, to be fully present. In the brief time she had spent with Billy, she wasn't racing ahead, she wasn't back in the past, thinking of all the negative encounters with Billy's family. She wasn't in her head overthinking everything he said. She was there with him and it was a gift from the great Spirit.

CHAPTER 8

Lucy checked the whereabouts of Rose's former boyfriend on the day that Rose went missing, and it turned out he had landed at Shawano Airport the day before with his father and brother on his father's private plane. But he had gone directly to St. Norman's and practiced the entire day. All of his roommates except Matt, who had not gotten to school yet, said Colt had been there the entire night.

Colt said he had no contact with Rose since they broke up in May. When Lucy asked why they broke up, Colt said it was because they both thought they were too young to be so committed and they wanted to see other people. He paused for a moment and seemed to be struggling about whether or not to say anymore.

"Are you holding back on something?" Lucy asked, picking up on the pause.

"Well, it's just that I have no proof," he said hesitantly.

"Proof of what?" Lucy asked.

"I kind of wondered whether Rose might have been experimenting with drugs," he continued.

"Why did you think that?" she continued.

"Toward the end of our relationship, she just seemed to drift away from conversations, and she would disappear for long periods of time. I would call her friends and none of them seemed to know where she was either," said Colt.

"Maybe she was just sensing the relationship was waning and was avoiding confronting the end with you?" Lucy offered.

"That's why I didn't want to talk about this with you, Officer Teller," said Colt. "It's just a feeling I had toward the end. It could have been a hundred reasons, but I suspected drugs."

"It would fit with some of the other things I've heard, that her grades had slipped, that she'd become more reclusive," Lucy wondered out loud.

Lucy then interviewed Colt's father on his next visit to Shawano when he returned a couple of days later to watch the first scrimmage at St. Norman's. He gave her every impression that a wealthy neurosurgeon should not have to waste his time being interviewed by some Indian cop.

"You can't even give me a traffic ticket," he said. "Why should I bother answering your questions about some girl who's been kidnaped?"

Lucy's first thought was to question why he assumed she was kidnaped, but she decided to just make a mental note of it.

"First of all, I'm not arresting you for anything," she said. "Secondly, if you'd prefer that I contact Agent Scruggs of the FBI who I closely work with, so that he can ask you the same questions, I'd be happy to do that. You know, as a man concerned with healing others, I thought you might want to help me locate a missing girl whose parents are frantic to find her," Lucy said, unable to control her sarcasm.

Lucy wasn't sure which of the points pushed him to reluctantly cooperate, but with a sharp inhale and exhale he started his recollection of the two days in question.

He had landed at Shawano Airport because it was more convenient than landing in Green Bay. They kept a car at Shawano because he flew up for all of Colt's games. He said he hung around to watch practice the next day and help his boys get settled for the year, then left Shawano Airport about 2 a.m.

"That seems quite late to start back to Texas," said Lucy.

Dr. Dickson looked at her with disdain and calmly replied, "I do brain surgeries that last 12 hours on little sleep. I can handle flying a plane."

Checking with the tower at Shawano, Lucy found that Dr. Dickson did leave at two. His flight log indicated no passengers, but he drove directly into his airplane hangar and took off. His log indicated he landed on the field behind his house. There was no one who could verify anything different.

CHAPTER 9

When they first started, Lucy thought they were dreams of her previous drug use returning. She was in a somewhat familiar out-of-control, dreamy, foggy and drug-induced coma-like state. She would wake up in a sweat and be so happy to find Ray by her side. She had married him shortly after he left Maehnowesekiyah after treatment for PTSD, which he developed after his last deployment to Africa.

His treatment continued for a while after leaving inpatient therapy. He had gotten very involved in a skill they taught there called mindfulness, a practice started nearly 2,000 years ago by Buddha. According to Jon Kabat-Zinn, mindfulness is awareness that arises through paying attention, on purpose, in the present moment, non-judgmentally. It was very helpful to his treatment, and when Lucy woke up from her dreams, he would coach her in focusing on her breathing. It was beautiful in its simplicity. She would focus just on breathing in and out. When her mind would wonder she just escorted it back to her breathing, and eventually she would fall back asleep.

Lucy and Ray had a daughter named Ava a year or so after they were married. She was a sweet toddler and a nice addition to the family.

Lucy began to be an expert at recognizing when Ray's PTSD symptoms would rear up. She started calling him "Raybo" after the movie Rambo, and it would bring a smile to his face. Soon Lucy's mother and his two stepchildren who also lived with them would do it as well. After being alone so long in life, Ray was just glad to be a part of it all and found that humor worked well at helping him to relax. Ava's version of Raybo turned out to be Rainbow. Nothing made him happier.

In spite of Ray's good work, the dream would return, and Ray began to explore with Lucy the idea that, in the culture of the Menominee, maybe her dream was more of a reworking of her previous life. She began to remember some of the subtleties of the dream. Unlike before, she didn't inject herself with a needle, but instead was injected by someone else whose face she couldn't see. During the dreams, she couldn't get out of bed and her head always hurt. She began to get up and write down new observations after each of the recurrences. The room was always the same. It was small and dark, there was a window, but the blinds were always drawn tight.

Once she remembered trying to get out of bed and noticed she had a catheter and one leg was restrained to the bedpost. Ray would usually be the first awake in the house. He would still have dreams of the horrors he saw in Africa. When he would wake, he developed a routine that helped him stay in shape, meditate and pray all at the same time. Like so many Natives, he was a hodgepodge of spiritual beliefs. Many of the native customs and beliefs had been literally been beaten out them in boarding school, and replaced with Christian beliefs.

Then he added Mindfulness. Like so many who practice mindfulness, it was easy for his mind to wander while just concentrating on his breathing. There was nothing wrong with that, because part of the practice is being non-judgmental. When he noticed his mind wondering, he was taught to just make note of it and slowly escort his thinking back to his breathing, but it frustrated Ray.

So, he slowly developed a routine that worked for him. He started by facing East and kneeling the way his Muslim brothers did in prayer. He found it was wonderful for stretching his legs and back. He then would pray, "Allah, Yahweh, God the Father, Son and Holy Spirit, Great Spirit, Creator, grant us peace, respect and understanding among our nations, races, religions and political parties."

Then he followed up with some other yoga stretches and 50 pushups before turning over on his back. After that, it was easier to concentrate on breathing and his heart rate as his body gradually returned to homeostasis or balance. He prayed for balance in his life or what his Navaho brothers called Hozro. Having PTSD, nothing was more important than balance. Physiologically, it meant that he needed balance between his sympathetic and parasympathetic nervous systems. In laymen's terms, the sympathetic was the fight-or-flight response. If it was too active, he would suffer from anxiety and anger. The parasympathetic controlled the relaxation response. If it was too active, he suffered from depression. If he dwelled on the past, he would be depressed; if he dwelled in the future, he would be anxious. It was the balance of the two responses and staying in the present that worked best for him.

He then would do more stretching, concentrating on his breathing and increasing the stretch as he breathed out. Then he did 50 sit-ups, breathing in as he lowered his back to the floor and breathing out as he raised his head to his knees. After that, he would do more mindfulness breathing and finally a prayer.

"Jesus, forgive me and help me to forgive others. Jesus, love me and help me to love others. Jesus, heal me and help me to bring your healing to all I come in contact with. God the Father, give me strength and courage, and Holy Spirit, give me understanding and the wisdom to use all of your gifts for a greater good."

He would end with 50 more push-ups, then lie quietly, even pausing his breathing for a moment in an attempt to quiet his mind and enjoy the peace that usually didn't last much longer. Soon other family members would begin to emerge from sleep. This time, the first one up was Lucy, who called his name with a mixture of fear and excitement.

"What's wrong?" he asked.

"I think Rose is alive," Lucy said. "Someone in the dream just called me Rose. It's not just about me. The spirits are trying to help me find Rose and I'll bet Scott Brandt is one of those spirits."

CHAPTER 10

Soon classes started for Ada, but since volleyball was a winter sport, her workouts were mostly in the weight room and runs of 5 to 10 miles. She did manage to spend time with Colt every day, and their relationship continued to progress. Colt took the minimum of classes in the fall because of football, and never seemed to need to study. The one time she suggested a date to the library, he brought his playbook to study and was ready to leave after a half hour.

By this time, Ada was crazy about Colt, and their only disagreements seemed to be Colt's increasing need to see her. He frequently cut class to be with her, and at football practice, wanted to be with her. While she wanted to be with him too, she took school and workouts seriously.

He also wanted her to spend the night at his place. but the rules of her dorm forbid it, unless they were going home for the weekend. By the time the first game came along, Colt played less than his best. Luckily, Corey had a great running game, and the Bolt twins made some great plays on kick returns and long runs after short passes, allowing the team to easily win.

Colt and Ada had dinner after the game. "I didn't play well today and it's your fault," he said.

Ada nearly chocked on the piece of chicken in her mouth, and her eyes grew wide. "My fault?" she answered with surprise.

"All I can think about is you, and us being together and you're not allowing that to happen," he said.

This isn't the way Ada had hoped it would happen. Things had progressed sexually with them, but up until now, Ada wasn't ready to go all the way. Colt hadn't hidden his frustration with that, but had let no be no. Ada had decided tonight was the night, but had hoped it could evolve and she wasn't pressured. "I…I…I think I'm ready," she stuttered.

Colt signaled the waitress to bring the check, even though they were only halfway through their meal.

When they entered his townhouse, all Colt's roommates were sitting around drinking beer and watching a movie. She had become friends with all of them and enjoyed their company, so she smiled and greeted them. She tried to sit down and watch the movie but Colt whisked her to his room. When he closed the door. he kissed her deeply and slowly lowered her to his bed.

She tried to slow him down and tell him she was uncomfortable with his roommates just outside, but he would have none of it, and she was naked in a matter of moments. As the passion built inside her, she soon forgot about Colt's roommates. Then she heard his voice in her ear.

"Aren't you excited?" he whispered.

"Yes," she whispered back.

"Then let me know," he said, the huskiness apparent in his voice.

Ada smiled and blew softly in his ear. "What would you like?"

"I want to hear you moan."

She immediately again became aware of his friends just outside.

"I want this just for us," she said.

"Do it," he insisted.

She moaned softly, but he wasn't satisfied. "Louder," he demanded.

The pleasure was gone for Ada now and from that point on, it was just an act to please the man she still hoped to care about, but from then on, she wasn't sure. She was thankful that his roommates were gone when she left Colt's bedroom.

CHAPTER 11

The next morning, Colt awoke to his brother Danny sitting next to his bed in his wheelchair. It was Sunday morning and in the distance church bells were chiming, but Colt knew Danny wasn't waking him for mass. He had a cup of coffee in his hand, and after Colt sat up in bed, he handed it to him.

"Where's the rest of breakfast?" Colt said with a smile, but Danny didn't smile back.

"I'm done lying for you," Danny replied.

"What's that supposed to mean?" asked Colt.

"I mean if you screw up with this girl, and something happens to her, look somewhere else for your alibi, because it won't be me."

"And then what will you do for a meal ticket?" Colt sneered.

"What will I do? You better start asking yourself what you'll do," Danny replied. "Ever since I got hit by that car, dad lost his vision of me playing in the NFL. Then he turned to you and my role changed to your support, and in some ways, that's the best thing that ever happened to me.

"So while you were in the yard throwing endless passes through a swinging tire, I was writing your papers and condensing information for your tests," Danny continued. "While you developed that right arm of yours, I developed a brain. I don't need legs to get a job, but what will you do if your dream of the NFL falls through? And judging from your last game, that's a real possibility."

"Wow, big brother found his voice," Colt replied. "But you still have to face the old man if anything happens to me."

"That doesn't frighten me anymore either, Danny answered. "Mom made a life for herself after she left dad."

"You mean after she abandoned us because she preferred booze," Colt replied. "And just remember that man raised us all by himself. And another thing, how do you know anything about our mother?"

"Let me take these one at a time," Danny responded. "You're a couple of years younger than me. I remember a mother that was kind and loving. You cried for days after she left. What I heard last night reminded me of what I heard growing up before we moved to the big house and I didn't have a bedroom next to theirs.

"Dad's control and abuse came first," he continued. "I know she became an alcoholic, and you can't blame that on Dad, but I don't know if she would have turned to booze in the first place if she weren't looking for a way to cope with him. I don't know what the truth is, because it's lost in history. I know what dad's side is because we heard it dozens of times: she was drunk and left for another man. Mom's side is the control and abuse were unbearable. She wanted a divorce, but wanted custody of us, but Dad said that if she wanted a divorce, she'd have to relinquish all rights to us and agree to never see or make contact with us til we were adults. I'm sure he thought she'd be dead by then.

"He had money; she had none. She agreed to divorce if he would give her updates on us, and give us the option to contact her once we reached 21. That answers your second question. I took that option expecting to have a brief conversation with a drunk. Turns out she went through rehab shortly after the divorce and she's been sober for 12 years. The old man kept his promise, probably to rub in what she's been missing.

"I care about Rose and now I care about Ada," Danny continued. "I don't know what happened to Rose, and I don't want to know, because then I'd be in more trouble than I am now, but I suspect since all of a sudden there are private conversations between you and dad that I'm not allowed to hear, both of you know stuff you're not telling."

"What do you want me to tell you?" Colt asked, his head now swimming with new information from his brother.

"Nothing. You just remember what I told you," he said, backing up his wheelchair and rolling out the door.

CHAPTER 12

That afternoon Colt got blindsided again. When he called Ada to find out what time they were getting together, she told him she had studying to do and was going to the union to hang out with her girlfriends later.

"How about you come over here and I'll help you study?" he asked.

"We've tried that before, and all you do is distract me," she countered.

"This time will be different," he said.

"I've heard that before. too," she replied. "I need to catch up on my reading and have a paper to write. Look, it's not just you. When you're around, I want to concentrate on you, not on Psych 100," she said, noting just the slightest insincerity in her voice that she hoped he wouldn't pick up on.

That seemed to appease him for the moment, and his brother's words about developing a brain rang in his ears.

"Okay, maybe I'll study some too, or watch some of the pro games on TV, but text me during your breaks," he said.

For the whole afternoon, Ada studied, wrote her paper and occasionally talked to Caroline, Rachel and Bobbie when she stopped by for a short visit.

His texts started about 15 minutes after they hung up. She answered the first one and then ignored the rest. *Still studying,* she responded after the fourth or fifth. She responded the same when he called her. When she put down her phone, a mixture of relief and dread filled her.

I DON'T LIKE BEING IGNORED soon showed up on her phone.

Sorry, she replied. *Do you want me to lose my scholarship and have to drop out of school? Then we'd never see each other.*

That would be great. Then you could move in with me and no longer have studies, volleyball or even your girlfriends come in between us. Just kidding, he added playfully.

That's where the dread comes in, Ada thought to herself. *I don't think you are kidding,* she said softly to the phone, and put it down without answering him.

The relief built as Colt got interested in a Packers game and she could actually concentrate. The girls studied all afternoon and took a break for dinner, then went back to their rooms and worked some more until close to nine when they all decided their brains were saturated and needed some fun while what they absorbed moved into long-term memory. They all laughed at that since memory was something they had been studying in Psych.

They stopped by Bobbie's room, and as timing would have it, she also decided she needed a break. When they got to the student union, they found lots of people looking for relief. The Bolt twins were in a corner with mostly other guys who were in heaven watching football through one eye and girls file into the union with the other.

"Hey," Eli said. "There's Ada without Colt attached to her hip. We better text him and tell him she's on the loose." They both smiled knowing how he was with the girls he liked. Always the instigator, Ethan took her picture and sent it to Colt. *Got this just before she was surrounded by men,* he texted.

That's when the texts and calls started on Ada's phone. The girls thought little of the first call when Ada left the table for a minute, or the first time her phone dinged with a text, but they noticed a change in Ada's response as they continued.

I hear you're out hunting men, the text read.

Just taking a break, she answered.

What about those slut friends of yours?

That's when she stopped answering.

When they stopped, Ada began to laugh and joke as she had earlier, until he showed up a few minutes later. Colt never came over to their table; he had no trouble mixing in with the guys watching the game, but Bobbie noticed that he rarely took his eyes off Ada and that his expression didn't look loving.

Caroline was the first to bring it up. "Can that guy ever let you out of his sight, or more accurately, his grip?" she asked.

"Suddenly, I'm feeling tired," Ada replied. "I think I'll turn in early. I hate to ask this, but could we all leave together? If I leave myself, he'll follow me out and there'll be a confrontation and I'm not ready for that now."

They all got out of their chairs and left together. Caroline scratched her face with her middle finger as they passed by Colt.

CHAPTER 13

There wasn't much to look at between Shawano and Green Bay as Lucy followed Highway 29, particularly once she passed Bonduel about 7 miles east of Shawano. The road was straight and there were corn and soybean fields that were sometimes visited by sandhill cranes, which were once again becoming more numerous in northern Wisconsin.

Lucy and Agent Scruggs discussed Rose's disappearance as they drove. Lucy told Scruggs what she knew, which wasn't enough to fill even a mile of the 31-mile trip. Lucy had no trouble with silence, but Scruggs was still getting used to Indian ways after spending his life dating white women who considered silence a sign that the relationship was not going well.

He took the opportunity to bring up a subject that was a major part of their relationship, but one that he and Lucy had never discussed.

"You know, it's interesting that one person's hero can be an other's villain," he remarked.

"What do you mean?" Lucy asked.

"Well, let's take John Marshal. He was a personal hero of mine. There's even a law school in Chicago named after him. To white America, he's right up there with George Washington. We owe him a lot, but most people don't know he made a whole different set of laws for Indians, and you're still stuck with most of them today," he continued.

"Then there was the Indian Reorganization Act of 1934 that gave Indians their own government, patterned after that of Washington D.C., with one catch: you'd still have to answer to Washington D.C. and the Bureau of Indian Affairs. That's why you have to drag me along whenever you want to investigate anything, even though you're twice the cop that I am. That's why the tribal police have to call in the sheriff's police to write a speeding ticket to a white speeder, even though the sheriff's police never saw the infraction."

"Well, you're right about Marshall," Lucy replied. "He didn't do us any favors, but there was a generous compliment in there that I don't want to slide by without thanking you and disputing it at the same time. I'm honored to ride with you."

"I just want you to know I'm here because the law demands it, not because I think you need me," Scruggs said. "If you excuse the expression, I'd kill to have your instincts."

"I'm sure Lieutenant Moon would be delighted if I had your knowledge of law and procedures, and I'd be in a lot less trouble with him that's for sure," Lucy added with a smile. "Besides, I need your input on this case. I have no witnesses, no trail to follow and no real suspects. All I have is a dream telling me Rose is still alive, but even that's short on details.

"In spite of my best efforts to recall every detail, all I know is Rose seems to be in a dimly lit room with a window where the blinds are always drawn. There's an attendant that always seems to be next to her, but I can't see her face. It seems to be a woman dressed in a nurse's uniform. Rose is restrained at her ankle but I don't know if that's to protect her or keep her captive, and it always seems she's frequently going in and out of consciousness. I'm starting to question whether the dreams are telling me anything or if it's just wishful thinking fueling my dreams," said Lucy.

"Well, they've been a valuable resource for you in the past, and since it's all we have, I don't think you should discourage the spirits by doubting them," Scruggs encouraged.

Soon they were entering Brown County and the newly finished road that allowed them to go right to Highway 41 and then to 72 that crossed the Fox River. Once on the other side, she took Webster past the prison with its high walls, guard towers and barbed wire. She crossed back over the river and soon was on St. Norman's campus. Lucy pulled the squad car in front of the student center and walked the steps and hallways to Bobbie's office. The door was open and Bobbie was alone. She knocked lightly and startled Bobbie, who in her mind was somewhere in Afghanistan looking for Austin.

"Can I come in? I need some serious help," Lucy said with a smile.

Bobbie jumped from her chair and gave her a hug. "You may be beyond my level of expertise, but I'll try to refer you to a whole team of competent docs," she said smiling back.

"Bobbie, you know Agent Scruggs, don't you?" Lucy said looking at the two of them.

"Are you kidding? He, Fiddler and Jesus are the only three people I know who rose from the dead," Bobbie said with a smile and shaking his hand.

Bobbie was referring to a time on the Rez when Fiddler pretended to kill a presidential candidate, then Fiddler and Scruggs pretended to shoot each other. It was reported that they were dead and the candidate seriously injured, all to give them time to find Fiddler's son who had been kidnapped. Ray was the one who found the boy and killed three men who were holding him captive. It was that incident that finally led Ray to seek treatment for his PTSD.

"Have a seat and tell me all about why you need help. I can at least listen," Bobbie said.

All of a sudden, the weight of Rose's case returned to Lucy and she slumped in the chair in a way that surprised Bobbie. Scruggs went to the window and watched the river.

"Wow, Lucy, you look like you really do need someone to talk to," she said.

"I really do, but it's is not so much about what's going on in my personal life as it is this case that has me stuck. Come to think of it, I guess it's my personal life too," Lucy said with a sigh.

Soon she had told Bobbie everything about Rose's disappearance, the dreams she'd been having, and why she was visiting the campus to talk with Colt and his roommates and any other friend of Rose's that might give her some insight about what could have happened to her.

"What does Ray say about the dreams? I suspect he may be telling you that you're getting too close," which was Bobbie's way of saying maybe you're too close, but Lucy caught it.

"Did I ever tell you that my dreams where instrumental in catching your brother's killers?" Lucy asked.

"I never knew that," Bobbie said, thinly veiling her surprise.

Lucy described her dream and how it convinced her that Bobbie's brother's death was no accident.

"That's what I get for allowing my counseling theories to get in the way of reality," Bobbie said. "What does Colt have to do with all this?"

"They dated for most of last year and broke up just before the end of spring semester," Lucy replied.

All of a sudden, the events of the previous Sunday evening flashed through Bobbie's mind. She thought of all the women she had worked with during her internship at the women's shelter. Bobbie could see the looks on their faces as they described the start of their relationships with their abusers. How they thought he was so romantic when he would send flowers, how he would always want to be with her, how cute they thought it was that he was jealous – even of her girlfriends.

It was only later that they realized that was the first signal of their wanting control – how they gradually separated them from their financial and emotional support systems. It was often only then that they realized they were trapped, and then the criticism and blame started, and soon the woman lost her self-esteem and believed she was lucky to have this man who beat her.

"Hey, Bobbie, are you still with me? Lucy asked.

Bobbie was startled for a moment. "Oh, yes, I find that if I mentally leave the room, it gives my clients time to think and solve their own problems. I also find that if I can make fun of how bad I am at counseling, it lets them know they can be incompetent and still survive."

Lucy laughed. "I know Colt is a big star around here, but I can't help but think he might be involved in this somehow."

Bobbie was about to tell her why Lucy might be right when she thought that maybe there were some ethical issues involved. Though Ada was never her client, she was part of her charge as a resident.

"I may have some information that may be helpful to you Lucy, but I need to talk with a couple of people first. Can you stop back after you talk with Rose's friends?"

"Sure," Lucy answered. Her spirits lifted ever so slightly.

CHAPTER 14

Lucy and Scruggs next stopped at Colt's townhouse. She parked the squad behind Colt's sports car and they walked to the front door and knocked. Colt answered wearing jeans but no shirt, socks or shoes. It was immediately apparent to Lucy that he was an athlete. He wasn't heavily muscled like a body builder, but he was chiseled like the statue David. His shirtless body not only revealed six-pack abs, but the low-cut jeans showed his oblique muscles running from the side of his groin. Colt showed no self-consciousness, but got immediately defensive like he did in football, and went right on the offense.

"What are you doing here?" he asked in a gravelly whisper. Without waiting for a response, he went on: "I have a reputation in this community to uphold and don't need some Native police car parked in front of my house."

"We still haven't found your ex-girlfriend, and though I know you were no longer seeing her when she disappeared, I was wondering if you thought of anything that might help us find her?" Lucy replied.

"I told you everything I know the last time we talked," Colt said. "If I think of anything else, I'll call you. Now get out of here before someone sees that car in front of my house."

"Well thanks so much for your hospitality," Lucy replied. "Are any of your roommates home? I understand they were friends with Rose as well, and maybe they'd be more interested in her welfare than in their reputations."

"They're all in class at the moment. Come back later, and when you do, park down the street," Colt said with the same cold, distant tone.

"Thanks, I think I'll just wait out front for them," Lucy said.

"This is harassment," said Colt, slamming the door.

True to her word, Lucy stayed in her car doing paperwork and talking to Scruggs until another car pulled out front. The first to arrive was Matt, carrying a bag filled with hockey gear and schoolbooks that looked heavy, though the way Matt wheeled it around, it could have been filled with balloons.

Lucy immediately leapt from her car. "I'll bet that bag is heavy, but you make it look like it's filled with helium," she said.

Matt looked surprised and a little scared. "Hi, officer. Was I speeding or something?"

"No, nothing like that," Lucy answered. "I'm Detective Teller from the Menominee Tribal Police, and that man just getting out of the car is Agent Scruggs of the FBI. I understand you were friends with Rose Waukau, who went missing this summer. I was hoping you could tell me something that might help me find her."

"Yes, I heard about that," Matt replied. "Of course, she was Colt's girlfriend, but she was around the house a lot, so I got to know her pretty well. I really liked her. I was shocked when I heard about it, but didn't she disappear from the Rez...sorry, the reservation?"

"That's okay, we call it that, too," Lucy replied. "Yes, she did and I learned from the others that you were still down in Chicago when it happened, but I was just wondering if you knew a place she might go to get away or hide out, even a place she said she always wanted to visit?"

Lucy could tell that Matt was busy searching his mind for anything that could be helpful, and Lucy couldn't help but contrast him to her conversation with Colt.

After a while Matt answered. "You know, I think even Green Bay was stretch for her. I always got the feeling she was most comfortable on the Rez." Matt smiled at Lucy's permission to use the word, somehow including him in her culture. "I don't know what happened to her, but I'm quite sure if she's hiding from someone or something, she'd find a place on the Rez to do it."

"Thanks, Matt," Lucy replied. "Did she ever describe such a spot?"

Again, Lucy could tell Matt was searching. "She once described the smudging ceremony to me and I know there was a tree where she always performed the ceremony, but I doubt that's a spot where she could stay for weeks or months."

"You're right, Matt. I have a tree like that too, but I'd need more shelter than that to stay for weeks."

"Did Rose ever tell you about anyone, like a family member, a friend, or even an acquaintance, that she didn't get along with, or seemed to have it in for her?" Scruggs asked.

Again, Matt thought before answering. "No, I can understand a lot of people, particularly women, who would be jealous of Rose, but she was so friendly that everyone seemed to like her."

"I wish I could help more. Like I said I really liked Rose. Did you talk to Colt?" Matt asked.

"Yes, but he didn't seem to want to cooperate much." Lucy replied.

"Well, I know he was pretty upset when they broke up. Colt isn't used to losing at anything, but he's moved on now has a new girlfriend, maybe even cuter than Rose if that's possible," he answered.

Just then Colt stuck his head out the door. "Matt, you don't need to talk to her. She has no jurisdiction here."

"But I do," Scruggs interrupted. "FBI." Scruggs shouted louder than he needed to while showing his badge to all the windows in the neighborhood.

Matt looked surprised. "She's trying to find Rose, I don't care about any legal stuff." That spoke volumes to Lucy.

"Thanks, Matt, I don't need to talk with you further. If you have the equivalent of the Great Spirit in your life, pray for Rose, will you?" Lucy asked.

"I'm not much into that, but I do wish for her safe recovery," he said.

Lucy talked to Eli, Ethan and Danny as they returned from class, and though they were respectful, Lucy got the feeling they had been pre-warned and each told the same story. They were all home that night drinking beer and watching movies.

Lucy asked what movie they had watched. *Rudy,* they all said, getting ready for football season. It amazed Lucy they would all have the same recollection about a night over a month ago.

"I understand Colt's father was around helping you get settled. Did he watch the movie with you, too?" she asked.

"Just for a little while, then he and I went to dinner," Danny answered.

"What about Colt, did he join you?" Lucy asked.

"No, he said he was tired and went to bed about the time we left," Danny said.

CHAPTER 15

While Lucy was away Bobbie was busy. First, she talked with her supervisor. She found out that since she had not learned anything about Colt from a counseling session, she was free to reveal whatever she felt was relevant to Lucy about him.

Second, since it was about a person who was potentially in danger, even if she had learned about it in counseling, she was obligated to share whatever she could that might save Rose's life. Bobbie's problem, however, was how little she really knew. Was she just projecting what she had learned in her internship onto Colt and Ada's relationship? After all, she was basing it on what happened in one night. Ada had never complained directly to her about Colt.

Bobbie decided to walk down to Ada's room and see if she happened to be there, and as luck would have it, she was. She knocked on the open door and the first thing she noticed was the flowers.

"The flowers are beautiful. Who are they from?" Bobbie asked.

"Colt," Ada said in a voice that indicated she did not want to pursue the flower thing further.

"Hey, mind if I come in and talk with you for a while?" she asked Ada.

"Not at all," Ada said with a smile, "but don't we have our roles reversed?"

"I guess we do, because I need to talk with you about a problem I'm having. It's a delicate one and I'm hoping I can count on you to keep it between us?"

"Sure," Ada answered with obvious curiosity on her face.

"My problem has something to do with your relationship with Colt, and I also need your permission to talk about stuff that is none of my business," Bobbie explained.

Ada sighed. "I've been trying to crank up the courage to talk with you about that anyway, so you've made it easier for me."

"Thanks, that helps me too," Bobbie said with relief in her voice.

"There are a number of events that have come together all at once, that involve you and me in a way I wasn't expecting, and right now they're all jumbled up in my head and I don't know exactly where to start," Bobbie began.

"Don't you people always say to start at the beginning?" Ada said with a smile, trying to add some levity.

"That's the problem," Bobbie said. "I don't know exactly where the beginning is, or at least which beginning. Okay, hell with it. What do you know about Rose?"

Ada looked surprised. "Not much – who's Rose?"

"For most of last year, Colt dated a girl named Rose, and right at the end of the year they broke up," Bobbie said. "This summer, right after football practice started, Rose disappeared and hasn't been heard from since. Not even a ping from her cell phone."

Ada was speechless.

Bobbie continued: "Now before you draw too many conclusions, Rose was Native American and disappeared from the Menominee Reservation thirty-some miles from here. Colt swears he was on campus and his roommates back him up."

"Colt has mentioned that he was in a relationship, but never mentioned a name," Ada said, still in shock.

"Today a friend of mine stopped by my office. Her name is Lucy Teller from the Menominee Tribal Police and our lives seem to keep getting intertwined. I had a brother who went to school not for from here. He was killed in an accident on the Menominee Reservation and it was Lucy who proved it wasn't an accident and brought his killers to justice."

"Wow, you never told me about that," Ada said, her head going from swimming to sinking.

"Here is where it gets even stranger and where you come into the story.

For my internship in counseling, I worked at a women's shelter. Are you familiar with what they do?" Bobbie asked.

"I've heard of them, they provide housing for women mostly who have been abused right?" Ada replied.

"Yes, exactly," Bobbie answered. "Well, the other night when we went to the union, I began to have flashbacks of what those women would tell me about their relationships, especially early in the relationship."

"What do you mean?" Ada asked.

"Well, how they would go out with their friends and how their abusers wouldn't leave them alone," Bobbie continued. "It was an early sign of how possessive and controlling they were, but at the time, they thought it was a sign of how much he cared for them and often thought it was flattering that he cared so much." Bobbie stopped to see what kind of reaction Ada had to that.

"Now this cop friend of yours shows up, and you're convinced Colt is an abuser and perhaps a murderer?" Ada responded defensively.

"I'm sorry, Ada," Bobbie replied. "I haven't drawn any conclusions; I'm just trying to sort out fact from fiction. I'm new at this, and I'm trying to keep from making the mistakes that so many people do when they get a little bit of knowledge that can be dangerous. You said you were trying to build the courage to talk with me about Colt. What are your concerns?"

"Sorry, I'm just confused," she said. "Colt has never laid a hand on me in anger or violence. I just know that at first I was wild about him and now I'm not so sure, but I don't think he is capable of hurting anyone."

"Have you thought about how you'll proceed from here?" Bobbie asked.

"Well, you saw the flowers? He apologized about the other night and promised it would never happen again," Ada answered, leaving out that he also apologized for making her uncomfortable during sex and promised that wouldn't happen again either.

The first part was already enough for Bobbie to get lost in the cycle of abuse and how apologies were usually followed by promises and a honeymoon period, but she cut off that thought and tried to stay in the present with Ada.

"So, it sounds like a part of you wants to continue, and I hope I'm not putting my thoughts in your head, but there's another part of you that's questioning that direction," Bobbie responded in her best counseling voice.

"That's true, but it isn't even so much about him," Ada replied. "I was looking forward to college being more carefree and all of a sudden this all seems way too heavy. I think I'll try to continue with Colt, but maybe to see if we can't go on a little more casually."

"Sounds like a plan for now," Bobbie responded. "But how about if we continue to talk about how it's going? I'll do my best to just listen and help you continue to sort this through based on how it goes."

With that. Bobbie gave her a hug and headed back to find Lucy waiting at her office door.

CHAPTER 16

obbie sat down in her chair with a thud and Lucy smiled. "I guess there are few people I'd rather get tangled up with than the Brandt family, but I really am sorry I keep doing this to you guys."

"We could never do enough for you, you know that," Bobbie said with a sigh. "I do wish, though, we could just get together for a fun social event sometime."

Lucy laughed again. "That does sound nice. How about dinner and ice cream out on the deck of Pine Hills Lodge before it gets too cold?"

"You're on," Bobbie said. "That makes me think it's been a while since I've visited my folks. I think I'll take a run up this Sunday for a visit. I'll check with them – maybe we could meet there for brunch on Sunday."

"Make sure to give them my best, and I'll check with Ray about our schedule," Lucy said with obvious affection in her voice. "Now, how can you help me with Rose's disappearance?"

"Well, I don't know if I'll be helping or only further muddying the waters," Bobbie said. "I've gotten to be friends with a girl Colt has been dating lately. She's tall and attractive and from what I can gather, looks similar in some ways to Rose. I've probably become closer to her than I should because she's a girl on my floor, and I suppose technically, she's in my care. Anyway, she and a couple of other girls from the floor and I went to the union the other night to take a break from studying and Colt would not let her alone. He kept calling and texting her all the while we were there, and finally, he showed up and kept staring at her the whole time. We finally got so uncomfortable we all left together."

Lucy looked skeptical. "So, they're young and in love."

"I know that's the conclusion most people would draw, but I worked at a women's shelter for my internship, and it just sent me back to how so many of the woman described the start of their relationships. I just got the feeling he was trying to discourage her from having a relationship with anyone else. You have your dreams and I have my intuition. I'm trying to learn how to trust it more," she said.

Now it was Lucy's turn to have to reconsider as Bobbie had with Lucy's dreams. She remembered what Rose's father had said about conversations with Rose on the phone – how Rose would end them as soon as Colt appeared.

"You know, I just remembered something Rose's father said about speaking to Rose on the phone and how she would end the conversation as soon as Colt came in the room. Maybe this is starting to make sense," she said.

Lucy started to laugh.

"Hey, do you think I can go to the D.A. with a combination of your intuition and my dreams?" They both laughed, neither knowing they might soon have more to go on.

CHAPTER 17

The following Saturday, Ada sat in the fourth row of the stadium next to Matt and a few rows up from Danny and his father. Colt liked them all to be together in the same spot every week so he could peek up while the defense was on the field. Even during warm-ups, his father seemed to have his eyes glued to the field and pretty much ignored Danny, who seemed to be used to it and was lost in his own thoughts.

It was a beautiful early fall day with blue skies and abundant sunshine. The stadium was large for a smaller school, but St. Norman's had a reputation for good football and there was no shortage of private donations. The crowd was beginning to file in, but there were mostly empty seats between the four of them.

Ada decided to take advantage of being with Colt's friend while Colt wasn't in earshot.

"I heard about Rose the other day," Ada said.

That got Matt's attention and it appeared that even Colt's father stiffened just a little.

"What did you hear?" Matt asked. trying to sound casual.

"Not much – just that she and Colt were an item and they broke up just as the school year was ending," Ada answered. trying to sound casual. "Why did they break up?"

"I really don't know, you'd have to ask Colt." Matt replied.

"What did you think of her?" Ada asked. deciding to pursue it just a little further.

"I liked her and miss seeing her," he answered. "I hope she's okay. I'm sure you learned she went missing."

"Yes, I'd seen some pictures of her around campus, but never dreamed I had even the slightest connection to her," Ada replied. "Now I know some of her friends are my friends."

Ada decided to let it drop since it seemed to make Matt uncomfortable and she got the feeling maybe Colt's dad was listening. He didn't seem to like her much anyway and she didn't need to make matters worse. Soon they were playing the national anthem and it gave them a chance to change their focus. Colt redeemed himself from the last game. His passes had pinpoint accuracy and he moved in the pocket. avoiding tacklers to give himself additional time to throw. Ada would look at his father with every completion and he beamed with pride.

CHAPTER 18

After the game, Colt hugged his dad in the middle of the field. In spite of what should have been a celebration, the words between them seemed heated and serious. That night Ada had dinner with Colt. As casually as she could she decided to bring up Rose.

"You know I've been seeing these pictures around campus of that missing girl, and I found out today that you dated her all last year?" she asked.

"What about it?" he asked, trying to sound matter of fact, but Ada noticed just a hint of threat in his voice.

"I was just surprised," she replied. "You know, you look at a picture of a missing girl and think it has nothing to do with you, only to find out that there's more of a connection than I realize."

"And what connection is that?" Colt asked, no longer trying to hide his irritation.

"Just that she had some of the same friends as me. Just like me she got to know your roommates, your brother, your dad, some of the guys on the team. I'm just surprised you or they have never brought her up before," Ada answered.

Colt seemed to realize he was getting defensive and when he spoke again, his voice was considerably softer.

"I guess what you said in the beginning is the reason," he replied. "That all happened before you got here, so why talk to someone about a person he doesn't even know? Who was it that talked to you about her?"

"It was my friend, Bobbie," she replied. "I guess she's friends with the cop that's investigating Rose's disappearance," Ada answered.

"Speaking of connections...why is it you're becoming friends with a woman who is supposed to be your surrogate mother and is nearly twice your age?" he continued.

Now it was Ada's turn to be defensive.

"She's only eight years older than me, and I think part of my attraction to her is she's older and wiser," Ada said. "I miss my mom a lot and Bobbie helps fill that void."

"Your attraction," Colt said mockingly. "Should I be concerned about what goes on with you two after I drop you off at night? Do I have competition?"

"I think we better change the subject," Ada said. "I don't like the way this is headed."

"Yeah, I guess I better get back and spend some time with my old man." Colt signaled the waitress for the check.

They drove back to Ada's dorm and she changed the subject to the game and the rest of the schedule. Colt jumped on the chance to talk about football, particularly when it was one in which he played particularly well.

They sat outside the dorm in Colt's car and kissed. Colt tried taking it further but Ada stopped him.

"There might be people watching," she said. "We don't want to appear on YouTube," Ada said smiling and trying to keep it light.

"And we don't want to make Bobbie jealous," Colt added sarcastically.

With that, Ada opened the door and said goodnight.

What neither of them knew was that watching them wasn't a possibility for Bobbie, who at that moment was wishing she was safe in her room instead of driving home.

CHAPTER 19

After the game on Saturday, Bobbie decided to go home and talk with her parents. Like her brother years earlier, she wanted to talk with her parents about something troubling her, and like her brother, she would be traveling through the Menominee Reservation to get home. Like her brother, she chose to take Highway 55 along the Wolf River. She had different reasons than her brother for her decision. Though she liked the scenery, she also liked to visit the place of her brother's accident and check to see if a now-grown Lisa, once her brother's student, still put flowers by the tree that Scott hit with his car.

But like her brother, there was a car waiting for her when she got near that spot. The car pulled out in front of her just like it had to her brother's, but luckily, there was some differences. The night her brother lost control of his car it had been snowing. Bobbie had already been slowing down to look for the flowers, and these men didn't seem to want her to hit a tree. Bobbie pulled into the slow vehicle lane hoping to just go around the car she thought was having engine trouble, but found a man blocking that as well.

When she came to a stop, the man who had been in front of her came to her window. He made a rolling motion with his hand. Bobbie lowered her window a crack and the man said, "Lower it all the way. I'm not going to hurt you, just want to give you some advice. Are you Bobbie?"

Bobbie shook her head yes in surprise.

"I understand that your brother came to a sad end at this spot. Is that right?"

"Who are you? What do you want and how do you know about my brother?" she responded, now more than a little irritated.

"None of those questions are important, but you can call me Alex," he replied. "The one question you need to be asking yourself is *Do I want to end up like my brother? Because like him, I'm sticking my nose in stuff that doesn't concern me.*"

"I've got another question for you," Lucy Teller said, startling the man. "Should you be threatening a young girl with a cop standing behind you looking for any opportunity to throw your ass in jail?"

The man recovered quickly and continued to face Bobbie. "I'm glad you're here, Officer Teller, because I hear you almost lost your whole family because you couldn't leave well enough alone with her brother. Now you want to go causing people problems over some girl who you think ran away. Well let me tell you something about that girl. There's a certain chemical she loves to stick in her veins, and she'll do anything – and I do mean anything – to get that chemical."

"Maybe I should arrest you and see if you know anything about the girl who ran away. What do you think?" Lucy asked. "If it's true about the chemical, I bet you're the one who supplies it."

"I think you would be wasting your time, and besides, the guys in the car behind you might have an opinion about that as well," he sneered.

Lucy looked behind her and at three men in the car on the road. They simply smiled and waved, but she was sure they had weapons close by.

"I'm heading back to my car now, unless you want to get into something you're not prepared to handle," he said.

The man started walking and Lucy followed behind him.

"You might be surprised what I can handle," Lucy said, keeping him between her and his buddies. "The only thing we know for sure right now is if trouble started, there would be one person dead for sure, and that's you. Besides, maybe I have back up."

"I doubt that, Lucy," the man said with confidence.

"That's Officer Teller," a voice said coming somewhere from the woods.

The man turned as much as he could while keeping his back to Lucy.

"Don't worry, you won't see me but you can be sure I have a gun trained at your head and I never miss," the voice continued. "I'm also pretty sure all the men in the car would be dead before they got a shot off."

The man said nothing more but hurried to the car as fast as he could.

Lucy watched the men leave and memorized the license plate. She knew all along she had no intention of starting trouble with Bobbie in the middle. Then Lucy went to Bobbie's car and saw her white face.

"Ah. I see now why they call you pale face," Lucy joked, trying to ease her fear and maybe reducing her own as well.

Bobbie smiled weakly. "Am I glad to see you," she replied.

"You're not the only one with intuition," said Lucy. "I swear I heard a voice from the past saying go where you found me. I thought my relationship with your brother had ended when I found his killers, but he seems to hang around."

Bobbie looked to the sky and quietly said, "Thanks, bro."

Lucy looked to the highway as she heard another car pass quickly. She couldn't tell who was inside but she didn't need to see. She also knew where it was going and where it would be parked. She would bet her life that it soon would be parked in an airplane hangar at Shawano Airport. As she replayed the scene that played out, she found it curious that the man who threatened Bobbie always kept his back to her.

"Did you recognize the man who spoke to you?" she asked Bobbie.

"I don't believe I've ever seen him before, but he sure seemed to know me and you," she replied.

Soon Ray emerged from the woods carrying his rifle that he still kept from his days as a sniper for the military. The men who left did not know how lucky they were; had trouble started, they'd all be dead. Ray just nodded at Bobbie and smiled at Lucy.

"We'll follow you to the end of the Rez," Lucy said. "You should be fine from there. By the way, we'll see you at Pine Hills at 11:00 on Sunday; I talked to your folks."

"Thanks Lucy," Bobbie said. "I'll feel better driving knowing you are behind me."

Ray and Lucy followed Bobbie as far as the Wild Wolf Inn right at the edge of the Rez. There they pulled in the parking lot and waited a while to make sure she wasn't followed. Bobbie made it home without further incident and gave her parents an extra-long hug when she saw them.

On their way back home, Lucy asked Ray if he knew the man who had been talking to Bobbie, but he didn't. They stopped at the station and ran the plates that Lucy had memorized. As it turned out, the car belonged to a student at St. Norman's. His name was Todd Brewster, an 18-year-old freshman. Lucy was quite sure that none of the people in the car were college students. She would check him out on Monday, but she also had some other leads to pursue. She need not have worried, for she would cross paths with the man again, and this time she'd see his face.

CHAPTER 20

Lucy, Ray and Ava met Bobbie, her mother, Molly, and her dad, Hank, on the deck of Pine Hills golf course and restaurant at a little after 11:00 the following day.

Ava chased one of the last Monarch butterflies of the season as the families exchanged hugs and sat at a table in the warm fall sun. The deck off the restaurant sat on one of the higher hills in the area, and they were the only people sitting on it this morning. They looked out on the golf course and surrounding woods, but they were paying attention to one another. They spoke first of the people who they knew in common.

First, there was Dr. Wolf, better known between them as Dr. Meany. That was the name Lucy had given him when she first entered treatment and he wouldn't give her enough pain medication, as she was sure she needed. The Brandts wanted to know if he still was exercising as much as he used to when he was training for a race that included about every form of self-propulsion known to man.

"He still would prefer to sit on his stationary bike than he would his desk chair, when he's charting in his office, and I still see him swimming in Legend Lake first thing in the morning in the summer, but I think he's slowed down some," Lucy said. "His wife, Gayle, is still doing well, and works at the tribal clinic."

Molly was the first to bring up the events of the previous day. "I can't help but be concerned about what's happening with our daughter," she said. "I don't want to go through what happened to Scott all over again. Burying one child is more than enough."

Bobbie looked at Lucy with a guilty look. "I tried to hide it from them, but they could tell the moment that I walked in the door that something was wrong. Besides, I needed to tell it to somebody because it all seemed so unreal. How did he know all that stuff? I could understand that they knew I had a brother who died, but the exact location and why he was killed? I just don't get it." Bobbie said, bewildered.

"I know the feeling," Lucy answered.

"Well, what can we do to protect her?" said Molly, stepping back in with the concern of a mother.

"Would you be willing to leave for school early tomorrow morning? We found out the owner of the car they were driving is from St. Norman's. I don't think he was there, but the car wasn't reported stolen, so I want to talk with him. I could follow you back and Ray could come with me. I think once you're on campus you should be safe. We can alert the campus police to keep an eye on you," Lucy explained.

"That sounds fine," said Bobbie. "This has to be related to Rose's disappearance, but how and why?"

"There is no doubt in my mind that Colt's father is involved in this up to his neurosurgeon eyeballs," Lucy said. "I think the fact that he was there yesterday in the background tells me two things I already knew about him: One, he has to be in control, and two, he's so arrogant he thinks he's above the law and some stupid Indian cop is never going to be able to get the goods on him.

"I'm also sure that if I go after him now, he'd be lawyered up and I could never get him for Rose's disappearance. I'm not even sure that he isn't the one who came looking for her in the first place, for breaking up with his superstar son. I need proof," Lucy said with desperation.

"Okay, we came here for a social visit. I have to catch you up on the rest of my family who are doing amazing things," said Hank, finally chipping into the conversation.

And for the rest of the time they shared stories and fun events. Ray spent most of his time chasing Ava, who kept running down the steps and playing on the putting green. When they left, there were hugs all around and Molly added, "You take care of my little girl and yourself, too."

"I will," Lucy assured her, not knowing just how difficult that might be.

Bobbie decided to stay in Shawano that night with Kathy and Brad. Kathy was Scott's girlfriend once, and Brad was his best friend since grade school. It also helped that Brad was a heavyweight wrestler in college and made her feel safe.

CHAPTER 21

Like the Brandts, Colt and Ada were also having brunch on Sunday morning. He was kind and charming. He dropped her back at the dorm so she could study and he could watch football. Then he picked her up for a bite to eat in the evening. They talked and laughed through dinner and Ada could feel the old feelings coming back again. He put his hand on her arm and she felt the electricity she had felt on their first date.

He paid the check, and they held hands as they walked to his car. As they drove out of the parking lot he headed toward his place.

"I need to go back to my dorm. I have my first big test tomorrow, and I have to review," Ada said with the feeling of fear returning when she saw the look on his face.

"So, what am I to you anymore – just a meal ticket? Someone who saves you from dorm food, but gets nothing in return?" Colt said in a different voice than he had used all day.

"So, what does that make me to you? Someone who puts out when she gets fed?" Ada shot back.

Colt pulled off the road into the parking lot of a business that was closed for the day. When he turned toward her and looked into her eyes, she saw something that stoked the fire of her fear.

He took her arm in a way that hurt her, but she showed no sign of it, not wanting to give him the satisfaction of knowing he could hurt her.

"First of all, you don't talk to me that way, and second, I think I have more than showed you that you are more to me than a roll in the hay," he said angrily.

Ada caught herself before saying anything else that would escalate the situation. "Colt, I care deeply about you," she said.

"Care deeply," he interrupted sarcastically.

"Please let me continue," she said. "I feel more for you that I ever have toward anyone, but I'm new at this and I'd like to go slow. I want to enjoy being in college."

"You mean you want to date around and have sex with a lot of different guys," said Colt.

"No, I don't mean that," she continued. "I mean I want to have fun with my girlfriends, I want to enjoy playing volleyball. Believe it or not, I like learning! I want to study and get as much as I can from my courses. I would be happy and honored to be your exclusive girlfriend, but I don't want you and I to consume all of my time and energy."

"This sounds like Rose all over again," he mumbled.

Ada heard him and another log was tossed onto her fear fire.

"Look, I'm not trying to be disrespectful," she said as softly and calmly as she could, "but maybe if you keep ending up in the same place with women, you have to look at your own behavior as well."

In a voice that sounded more like a growl with eyes that matched, he told Ada to stop being a shrink like her lesbian girlfriend.

"Look, maybe we should just give this a rest for tonight," she suggested. "Why don't you take me home and we'll talk in the morning."

"Why don't you just walk home and we'll talk when you're ready to commit to this relationship like you should," he replied.

Ada started to protest when he reached over and opened her door, and shoved her with his foot. She decided to take her chances with the cold, dark, night air.

Colt sped off, and as soon as he was out of sight, Ada called Caroline. She borrowed a friend's car and Caroline and Rachel picked her up at a café she had walked to. When she got in the car she cried.

CHAPTER 22

The next morning, as they were getting ready to meet Bobbie, Ray and Lucy walked out their front door and found a note stabbed to it. The note appeared to have blood on it. It read: *Remember, you have three children now. If you're are both gone, can your mother protect them?*

"You're going to have to follow Bobbie on your own, I'm taking this note to Lieutenant Moon after I get the kids safely to school, and I'll take Ava with me to the station," Ray said.

"That sounds like a plan, but remember, they're just trying to scare us, Rainbow," Lucy said, seeing the rage build in Ray's eyes.

"They can't fuck with my family like this. I should have killed them all when I had the chance," he said in a low gravelly voice Lucy had never heard before.

She put her hands on his shoulders and looked him in his eyes. What she saw was frightening. She wondered if they knew what he had done to the last group of men who threatened a child.

"Promise me we will handle this together," she said. "I know how you get when any child is threatened, and these are your children, but if you act without proof I will lose you to prison and I can't handle that."

Ray's eyes softened just a bit. "I promise, unless they try something," he said.

Lucy left Ray with her mother and the children. She knew they would be safe but the Great Spirit help anyone who tries to harm them. She knew this was dangerous for Ray's recovery from PTSD, and even for her own. She just realized it had been a while since she made a meeting or talked to her sponsor. She would have to do something about that when she got home tonight, but then decided to call her sponsor right then and made plans to meet her that night.

She stopped in to say hi to Kathy and Brad and then she and Bobbie left for St. Norman's. They drove out Green Bay St. to Highway 47, took a right and drove a couple of miles past small factories and took a left onto the entrance ramp of Highway 29, even though had limited access, so besides an occasional cloverleaf, there are also some cross streets where cars trucks and farm equipment can go from one side straight across to the other. It was at one of these points near Pulaski that a pickup truck pulled in front of Bobbie and stopped on the highway. Bobbie slammed on her brakes, and just as she was about to hit it, the truck sped away.

Lucy had been lost in thought about what might be happening at home, and was jolted into the present in a hurry. She was just about to give chase to the pickup when she realized that would leave Bobbie alone. She wisely pulled off the road, and Lucy pulled behind her.

She stopped for a moment to collect her thoughts and that's when it hit her. Just because Kane and some of his friends were in jail for the murder of Scott Brandt, that didn't mean his operation had ceased to exist. That's why that guy kept his back to her. On her visit to Kane's place, once she saw a number of guys in the house. That's how they knew all about Scott.

Again, her impulse was to rush right over there, but it also hit her how Colt's father was involved and if she did that it might spoil his plans and he would have to figure a Plan B. It also hit her how the thugs got the car and probably the truck they were threatening Bobbie with. So Bobbie looked surprised when Lucy approached her car with a smile.

"I'm glad you find this amusing," she said. "I happened to be scared to the point where I don't know if I can drive another 15 miles to campus."

"I'm sorry about what happened just now, but you'll be happy to know I think I figured out who those men are and how they know about you and Scott. I'm smiling at my own stupidity. I can also tell you I think this could all be over soon. I'll contact an officer I know in Pulaski. He'll drive you to campus, and I'll drive him back on my way home," Lucy said.

Lucy radioed the Pulaski police and explained what had happened and they said they would send two officers right out and one would drive Bobbie's car to St. Norman's. While they waited for the other officer, Lucy called Ray and after asking how things were going and finding out there were no new developments, she asked him to wait on talking to Lieutenant Moon because she had some things she might be able to add. Just then, the two officers pulled up and she said she would fill him in as soon as she got home, but had to talk with a few people at St. Norman's and then stop in Shawano first.

CHAPTER 23

After arriving safely at St. Norman's, Lucy asked Bobbie if she would accompany her to visit Todd Brewster, whose car was used to stop Bobbie on the Rez. Bobbie declined.

"I'll confront him about it, but I need you to help me get him into treatment, and you know a lot more about that than I do," said Lucy.

Bobbie looked surprised. "How do you know he needs treatment?"

"Well, I don't know for certain," Lucy replied. "I'm trying to use my intuition like you do."

"I do know that sometimes intuition is wrong," Bobbie answered. "What if he's some kind of gangster?"

"Intuition should be backed up by some kind of facts, don't you think?" Lucy asked with a smile. "We do know he's an 18-year-old St. Norman's student. That doesn't prove he's not a gangster, but I'm pretty sure we'll know right away. We'll take campus security with us as well, to make sure we can get in his room."

Lucy, Bobbie and a campus cop named Russ went to a freshman dorm, but before they could knock on the door, they saw paramedics carrying someone out on a stretcher. The paramedics had already administered Narcan and the young man was awake, but was on his way to the hospital for observation. Lucy showed her badge and asked the paramedics if she could ask him a few questions, but they said she'd need to wait until he was safely at the hospital and in an assigned room.

Lucy turned to Russ. "I don't think this overdose was completely an accident," she said. "I think the people who sold it to him may have known he might be talking to us and didn't want him around to do that. Could you follow the ambulance to the hospital and make sure they don't try again?"

Russ nodded and left for his patrol car. Lucy looked into his dorm room and saw his roommate sitting with his head in his hands. She walked in and introduced herself and Bobbie before asking his name.

"James," he said without looking up. "I knew this was a mistake from the beginning. I asked for a transfer the first week of school, but they said I should try it for a while. Of course, I didn't tell them that this kid was on heroin and that's why I wanted out, and that there were strange characters coming up to him and taking his car. Now I come in and find him overdosed and have to call 911. What if I hadn't forgotten a book? I would have walked in and found him dead, for God's sake!"

Bobbie found an opportunity to change the focus, and replied, "James, you saved his life, and maybe started him on a road to recovery. You can feel proud of yourself."

For the first time, James looked up from his hands. "I sure hope you're right about the recovery part. I knew him in high school, but we really weren't friends. He was a baseball pitcher and was a sure thing to get drafted into the majors. Then he hurt his arm and lost his whole senior year. He had surgery and the docs put him on painkillers to help manage the pain. After that ran out, he missed the high they gave him and he was so depressed about missing his chance at stardom, so he started on heroin. I read that that's happening a lot with young athletes.

"He was so sure he'd be playing baseball that he didn't focus much on academics," he continued. "The coach here said he'd give him a shot if his arm healed, so he asked me to room with him to help him study, but it was obvious right off the bat that heroin had its hooks in him. He started missing classes and hooked up with these guys, and before he knew it, he was in debt and they would borrow his car for long periods of time. I know he wondered what they were doing with it."

"Do you know if they had it last Saturday?" Lucy asked.

"Yeah, he was a good guy and he'd do anything for anybody," James answered. "He told me I could use it to go to the game, but when I went to the parking lot to get it, it was gone. I told him and he said they must have had a key made one of the times they borrowed it. I could tell he hated the fact that he was trapped in this cycle but didn't have a clue how to get out of it."

"Do you know if his family is aware of any of this?" Bobbie asked.

"They'd put him in treatment before he got here," James said. "It's one of the reasons I agreed to room with him. But I hear him talking to them on the phone and he put up a good front. Will they know what's happening now?"

"I'll make sure they know all," Bobbie said.

"And you can add that there are criminal charges pending as well," Lucy added.

"My guess is you'll get your wish about the roommate situation," Bobbie said. "I would think once he's out of the hospital, he'll go right into treatment."

"If I can stay in this room and he gets treatment, I might be willing to give it another try with him, but only if he's clean and those guys aren't around anymore," he said. "Speaking of them, will they be coming after me because I told you all of this?"

"I'm hoping they'll all be in jail soon, and that's something else for which you can be proud," Lucy said.

James smiled. "I was exploited by bullies all through school," he replied. "It feels good to get back at them a little and help a friend at the same time."

After they left James, Bobbie said to Lucy: "Boy, you sure called that one. How did you know he was on heroin?"

"It's a favorite trick of pushers to take the car of someone indebted to them when they're about to do something illegal, so no one can trace the car back to them," said Lucy.

"I have to talk with my supervisor to find out if we can contact Todd's parents and who should do it," said Bobbie. "I'll let you know if I run into a problem."

"Could you do me one more favor, Bobbie?" Lucy asked. "I'd like to talk with Colt's brother, Danny. Could you get me his cell phone number from Ada? Maybe we can we come up with some sort of excuse as to why we want it. I don't want this getting back to Colt," Lucy said.

"Sure, Danny plays wheelchair basketball," she said. "I'll just tell her I have a new recruit for their team that would like to talk with him."

Bobbie called Ada and soon had the number. Lucy called him and he said he was at the gym and she was welcome to come over.

CHAPTER 24

Lucy met Danny at the gym. He was doing bench presses with three 45-pound plates on each side.

"That's pretty impressive," Lucy said. "I notice you don't have clamps on the end of the plates. Do they ever fall off when you aren't pushing evenly?"

"You're quite observant, officer," Danny answered. "I do that on purpose because sometimes I like to come here late at night and work out, and if I ever can't get the weight up on the last rep, I can just turn my upper body and they fall off, so I can return the bar to the rack. But I doubt you came here to learn my rather unusual workout practices. What can I do for you?"

"You're right," Lucy replied. "I just get the feeling that your brother and father are keeping you in the dark about what they're up to as far as Rose is concerned. I think they're doing that because they know you're different from them, and perhaps unlike them, have integrity. I believe Rose is still alive and they know something about how to find her."

Lucy went on to tell him about the events of the last couple of days.

Danny listened patiently as she told him about her and Bobbie's encounters with the drug dealers and about Todd's overdose.

"I think it's time I gave my father a call," Danny said. "I doubt whether he'll be straight with me, but maybe between talking to him and checking email and texts between him and Colt, I can learn some things. I'll get back to you, Officer Teller."

Later that day, Danny called his father, and just as he suspected, his father told him he was as crazy as that stupid Indian cop who was filling his head with nonsense.

Later that night he returned to the gym to finish his workout. He was alone as he often was. The man who entered the gym after him was no stranger to gyms. Like Danny, he had a large chest that no shirt could hide. He wore a sweatshirt with the sleeves ripped off, exposing his large arms. His legs, like Danny's, were much smaller than his upper body, but unlike Danny, he could walk.

The man who entered after Danny didn't carry a gun or try to cover his face, which was one of his two mistakes. Ray Waupoose had told Kane, his predecessor, that like Custer, he had underestimated his enemy. He thought he'd have no trouble handling a paraplegic on his own. His second mistake was unlike Lucy Teller, the man hadn't noticed that Danny didn't have clamps on the end of his weights.

"You need a spotter?" he asked, approaching Danny. "That looks like a lot of weight."

"No, I'm fine," Danny replied. He thought about mentioning that he could roll the weight off if necessary, but something made him hesitate. The man stood behind him anyway.

"Hope you don't mind if I watch," he said. "I can't believe you can do this. How many reps do you do?"

"Five," he lied. He normally did 10 repetitions, and wondered why he didn't trust this guy, possibly because he'd never seen him in this gym before. As Danny lowered the weight for the fifth rep, the man pounced. It worked for a moment while Danny got over the shock and surprise of what was happening. He was immediately filled with a sadness, realizing that his father had stooped so low as to hire a hitman so that Colt's football career would not be interrupted. He soon realized that this was no game as the man rolled the weight toward his throat.

CHAPTER 25

After Lucy left Danny, she decided to stop by the Launching Pad Restaurant in Shawano. It happened to be right across the street from the Shawano Airport, and was a popular night spot in Shawano. She and Ray liked to take the family there, particularly on the fourth of July, because there were fireworks right across the street at the airport.

She knew some of the wait staff and decided on a long shot that they would remember seeing Dr. Dickson's car coming and going the night Rose disappeared.

She walked in the door and was immediately greeted by Cindy. They had become friends while they were both taking courses at the College of Menominee Nation. Cindy was taking courses there because her folks couldn't afford to send her away to school, and besides, she was a little unsure about what she wanted to do in terms of a career. The only thing she knew for sure was that she was tired of struggling to make ends meet, and hoped to find some guy who was rich so she could have the lifestyle she knew she deserved.

In her case, that wasn't out of the realm of possibility: she had long, dark hair, a petite body, an engaging personality, and a gorgeous face. She had a long line of pursuers, but most didn't have the criteria high on her list: lots of money, so she spent her time working at the Launching Pad while she waited for Mr. Right to walk in the door.

As soon as Lucy saw Cindy, she kicked herself for not thinking of it sooner, because if there was anyone who would keep track of Dr. Dickson, it would be Cindy.

"What brings you in here without that cute family of yours?" Cindy asked.

"I'm here on business, and you might be just the person I'm looking for," Lucy replied.

"Whatever it is, I didn't do it," Cindy said with a smile.

Lucy laughed. "No, I'm wondering if you ever noticed a very expensive-looking BMW coming and going from the airport – probably parked in the airplane hangar. It would probably leave on a Friday night and return on a Sunday, especially during the fall."

"Are you kidding?" Cindy answered. "That's Dr. Dickson's car. His kid is the quarterback for St. Norman's. Some think the Packers may even draft him next spring. They come in here every once in a while and have a cup of coffee before heading back to Texas. I do my darndest to start a conversation with them, but the only one who doesn't turn up his nose at me is the guy in the wheelchair."

Lucy nodded. "Did you read about the girl who disappeared from the reservation this summer?"

"I did, and I almost called you about that because I also heard that she dated Colt," Cindy answered. "That night, the good doctor's car pulled into the airport about 9 pm – I know because I was playing volleyball outside and I was hoping he'd notice me in my shorts and tank top and stop to watch us play for a while. I noticed that he came back out of the airport again, which he never does, but instead, he sped off and I never saw him come back, and I was here til almost midnight. I didn't think too much more about it til I heard about Rose's disappearance on the radio. Then I decided someone with all that money would never stoop to anything so seedy."

"You might be surprised at what rich people are into these days," Lucy said.

"So, you think he might be involved in her disappearance somehow, and that maybe I'll have to visit him in prison?" Cindy asked.

"I have no idea – I'm just following possibilities," Lucy responded. "Besides, isn't Dr. Dickson kind of old for you?"

"When he has that kind of money, fancy cars and private planes, and can afford to commute here from Texas every week, he isn't old – he's distinguished," she replied.

"Well I wonder if you would do me a favor the next time Mr. Distinguished comes into town," Lucy asked. "Would you give me a call when he leaves the airport?"

"Sure, I'll tell the girls here to call me in case I'm not working. Then I'll call you."

CHAPTER 26

Once he realized what was happening, Danny let a wide smile creep across his face, which surprised the man. He rolled to his right, and with that, 135 pounds fell off the bar, which immediately jerked the bar in the other direction, sending another 135 pounds crashing to the floor. Now it was the man pushing down on the bar and Danny pushing up, and despite gravity and a 50-pound bar to his advantage, the man on top was no match for the man below, and the bar began to rise.

Danny realized that the man's hands lined up with the bars on the bench that held the weight when they were in a rest position. Now instead of just pushing up, Danny pushed toward the back of his head and the man's hands were crushed between the barbell and the support bar. He screamed in pain and let go of the bar.

Danny was now not only free, but he also had a weapon. In one motion, and still holding the bar, he sat up and twirled to face the man. The man was on the defensive and realized he was lesser person in the fight – even with two good legs. He got behind Danny's wheelchair and thought about pushing it toward him to see if he could knock him from the bench. Then from the corner of his eye, he saw a figure coming toward the door. He turned over the wheelchair and ran out the door, just as Matt was walking in. The man thought he would overpower Matt, who he outweighed by at least 50 pounds, but being used to body checks, Matt turned and the man flew sideways.

"What's his problem?" he asked his friend, and then remembered something else. "Hey, I thought we were going to work out together?" Matt said turning his attention to his friend.

"Sorry, I forgot," Danny said. "I'm feeling a little lightheaded." He dropped his head between his knees.

Matt rushed over and the events of the last few moments began to catch up with him in his head.

"Heeey...who was that guy who came rushing out of here, and what was he doing with your wheelchair?" he asked.

"He was my assassin, but luckily he wasn't that good at it," Danny replied.

Matt stood for a moment in silence. "You mean he was trying to kill you?" he asked in astonishment. "You're one of the best people I know – who would want to kill you?"

"Thanks for the compliment, Matt, but my father only values people who are whole in his narrow estimation," he replied.

"This time the silence lasted longer and Matt swallowed hard. "You mean your father is trying to kill you?"

Danny couldn't answer but just nodded.

"As hard as this may be, you can't say anything to Colt or any of the roommates," Danny said. "I have to help gather some evidence for Officer Teller. She's convinced that Rose is still alive, and that my father knows where she is."

"You've got my word," Matt said. "How can I help?"

"I'm afraid he may come back with friends, so we need to get out of here, but I don't want to go back to our place," he said. "Let's meet at Lombardi Hall. It's time the girls knew what they're dealing with."

CHAPTER 27

anny and Matt each drove to the parking lot outside Lombardi Hall and took the elevator up to Bobbie's room. They were surprised that Russ, a campus cop, was in the downstairs lobby and asked them to hold the elevator. He asked casually who they were visiting, and when they said Bobbie Brandt, his demeanor changed and he became much more official.

"Do you have business with Miss Brandt, or is this just a social call?" he asked.

"Well, a little bit of both," Danny said.

"Does she know you're coming?" he continued.

"No," Matt said, slightly irritated with the interrogation.

"It's kind of late. Maybe this could wait until morning?" said Russ, sounding a little more like a concerned father.

"Look officer," Danny continued, "we think Bobbie and some of the girls on her floor might be in some danger and we just want to warn them. You're more than welcome to listen in on what we have to say, and as a matter of fact, maybe you should."

"Miss Brandt is already aware of that," Russ replied. "That's one of the reasons I'm hanging out in her dorm." Russ knew he had said too much.

"We didn't know that, officer, but we may be able to shed some light on what's going on here," Matt said. "Just let us knock on Bobbie's door. If she doesn't answer or says she doesn't want to talk with us, we'll leave and you can escort us to our cars. If she does, we'd like to include three of the girls from her floor as well. Perhaps we may want to conference in Officer Teller from the Menominee Tribal Police."

"What a coincidence, I just met her this morning," Russ said, kicking himself again.

They were now standing outside Bobbie's door. "I think it would be best if you let me talk to her first," Russ said. "She's has had a lot thrown at her in the last couple of days, and she's a little spooked."

Russ knocked on the door. It took a few moments, but Bobbie's voice came from the inside.

"Who is it?" she asked, her voice shaking ever so slightly.

"Bobbie, it's Russ from the campus police," Russ answered. "There are two men out here who want to talk with you. They say they have some information that might shed light on what's been going on with you and Officer Teller."

"Who are they?" Bobbie asked.

Russ' face turned red, realizing he hadn't asked their names.

"I'm Danny Dickson, Colt's brother, and my friend is Matt, Colt's roommate," Danny replied.

To the surprise of the three men, there was already a conversation going on inside the room.

"Russ, I'm going to open the door and let them in, but you may compromise your job if you hear what they have to say," Bobbie said. "If you want, you can wait in the hall and guard the door."

Russ knew that Dr. Dickson had contributed a significant amount of money to the school and that Colt was the starting quarterback. He decided he'd talk to his supervisor first, and knew he could always learn what he needed to know from Bobbie.

"I'll keep an eye out here," Russ said.

As it turned out Ada, Caroline and Rachel were already inside Bobbie's room. They called Lucy and spoke her on the speaker phone. Lucy had just returned from the Launching Pad, so all of them had much to contribute to the conversation. Each shared what the last 48 hours had produced.

"Okay, I have a feeling that the pressure is on for Dr. Dickson to make a move with Rose," Lucy started. "I believe she's still alive but if he has anything to do with containing her, he's going to have to make sure she doesn't survive, and her death has nothing to do with him. We have to know his plan and how to stop it. You all know what has happened over the last 48 hours and know that all of your lives are in danger. I wouldn't blame any of you for dropping out of this, but promise me you will do nothing to inform Colt of what's going on. I don't know what his part is in this, but I do know he is loyal to his father.

"Ray and I will go and talk to our supervisor tomorrow and see if I can't get permission to fly to Texas with a subpoena to search his house, but that's a long shot. I don't want any of you to put yourselves in danger, but anything you can learn to save Rose's life, I sure would appreciate knowing."

"Let's get the son of a bitch," Caroline said.

"Now remember, no heroics," Lucy reminded them.

"I'll call my mother," Danny offered. "She probably knows my dad the best, and she still lives in the area. Maybe she can help."

"I suppose I could call Colt," Ada said. "I can tell him I've had a change of heart and want him back. Maybe I can learn things form him."

"Over my dead body," Caroline said. "The first thing he's going to do to make you prove your commitment is make you sleep with him and that would be degrading and disgusting."

Everyone agreed.

"He may call you and apologize again," Bobbie said. "Tell him you need time and talk to him when he calls, but that's it."

CHAPTER 28

The next day Lucy and Ray met with Lieutenant Moon at the Tribal Police station. From the time she was a rookie, she was intimidated by the man. It's not that he was that big or physically intimidating, he never got in her face and yelled, and he didn't call her names. It was just the look of exasperation and pain when she screwed up or did things without authorization, both of which happened frequently.

Lucy was tired of disappointing him. He had told her over and over again that she was a good cop, but she could tell that he didn't understand her ways. Sometimes he would refer to them as the old ways. There was a time when the Menominee were proud of being the people of dreams, he would say, but now they had to use modern police work to discover guilt and innocence.

Lucy and Ray did their best to present the evidence they had against Dr. Dickson. His eyes closed for a long time as Lucy cringed and said she dreamed Rose was being held in a room, that she was being given medication both by mouth and injection. Then it was Lieutenant Moon who cringed as he asked, "Did you see who was giving her the pills and injecting her in your dreams?

"Not very clearly, but it appears to be a woman's hands that are doing it," Lucy answered.

"Yet you seem convinced that it's Dr. Dickson who's holding her captive?" Moon asked with his eyes closed tighter than ever.

"Well he's a rich doctor; he wouldn't be injecting her himself," Lucy countered. "Besides, there's more. When Bobbie was threatened by those men, he drove by right after they left."

"Yes, you said that earlier, but what you mean is a car *like* his drove by," Moon said. "You said you didn't get a good look at who was inside. And does this mean you're again using the Brandts to do police work?"

"No…well, yes…maybe a little, but it's not like I deputize them or give them guns," Lucy replied. "It just seems to happen that they wind up in the middle a lot, and they always end up being so helpful."

"What about the note on our door that we showed you?" Ray asked.

"Don't get me wrong – I know that Rose disappeared under strange circumstances, and I believe there are bad men out there who have it in for you and Lucy," Moon replied. "It's just that there's very little true evidence to point in any one direction. Ray, you and I have always pretty much agreed on things, then you got involved with Lucy and now you seem to have gone over to her side, so to speak?"

"I don't always understand Lucy, sir," Ray replied in a calm and steady voice, "but I trust her and it's been demonstrated to both of us that she's usually right."

"I agree," Moon said, "but let's back up a little bit and review the case. Lucy, you said you had the whole house dusted for fingerprints?"

"I did, but they didn't come up with much," Lucy answered. "There are no matches for either Dr. Dickson or Colt on file, and even if we could get a match for Colt, he had visited the house before."

"What about the car?" Moon asked. "I understand that her folks got her that this summer, which would have been after the two broke up. And maybe whatever happened took place before Rose ever got in the house."

Light bulbs went on in Lucy's head, and again, she had to admit she made another rookie mistake. "But we still wouldn't have a match."

"Didn't you say the brother who had an attempt on his life was willing to cooperate?" Moon asked. "Maybe he could get a glass that Colt uses and give it to us in case we find a print on the car we can identify."

"What a great idea!" Lucy replied. "There's a reason you've moved up the ranks, Lieutenant," Lucy said.

Moon again closed his eyes. "And there is a reason I made you a detective Lucy, because even though we don't often agree, I know you and I come to the same place in the end."

"Lieutenant, my only concern is that the pressure is mounting on Colt and his father," Lucy replied. "I know I can't prove it, but I'm sure that the attempt on Danny's life happened because he confronted his father about Rose. I think he has to do something soon and I believe he means to kill her in a way that doesn't implicate him or Colt. I think that's why he's employed the help of the drug dealers that took Kane's place."

"Well, it would make sense, that if he's keeping her in Texas, he would want to get rid of her around here, and perhaps that would explain the injections she's getting in your dream," Moon replied. "He could bring her back here and put her in some sleazy motel and inject her with an overdose."

Just then Ray spoke up with more enthusiasm than he usually showed.

"I just had another thought," he said. "The Doc probably doesn't want to kill her, although Rose might wish she were dead. What if they could prove she was alive like on a video with either a newspaper or a news broadcast in the background, and then use their drug network to transport her to another country?"

Lucy cringed. "You mean like white slavery?"

"Yes."

"And he could use these drug dealers to do it to keep those valuable surgical hands clean. And in his mind, he's even living up to some sick notion of the Hippocratic oath," Ray said.

Moon again shut his eyes. "You two just get further out there. Didn't you say that waitress was going to call you when the doctor's in town next? Maybe we could have the Shawano police stop him for a routine traffic stop and if the girl is in the car, they could arrest him on the spot."

"Thanks, Lieutenant," Lucy said. "I'll get right to work on those fingerprints."

As soon as she left, Lucy asked the lab tech to go back out and dust the car. Then she called Danny and asked him to discreetly get a glass that Colt had just used and bring it to the station. She called Cindy and told her she expected Dr. Distinguished to be coming into town in the next couple of days.

When she arrived back home and got out of her squad, Willy waived from his house and headed toward her. She waited in her driveway and he soon stood in front of her. When he got closer, she noticed he sported a black eye.

"Did you run into a wall?" she asked.

"No, actually it was my dad's fist," he said casually.

"What was that about? Do you want to press charges?" Lucy asked.

"No, he is what he is," Willy replied. "I'm used to him. I just wish he would leave my mom alone, but I'm here to talk to you about something different. The other night, I heard Buck barking before dawn. That's not unusual, but he sounded more serious than usual, so I decided to check it out.

"I saw two men approaching your house, and I snuck over and get a closer look. I saw them stick something on your door, and then sneak away. I knew you weren't in immediate danger, so I just memorized their faces and went home and drew them."

He then handed Lucy a couple of scraps of paper.

She glanced at them not expecting much, but then her eyes nearly popped out of her head. She had seen a number of police sketches in her day, and these were better than most.

"Wow!" she exclaimed.

"So, you know them?" he asked, sounding surprised.

"I think they may have been in the car that I had a run-in with the other day, but I'm amazed at how good these sketches are. Where did you learn to do this?" she asked.

Willy smiled. "I took a couple of art classes at school, but mostly I taught myself."

"How about if next semester you take some classes at College of Menominee Nation, and if there's a cost, I'll pay it," she offered.

Willy just looked at her like she'd grown an extra eye on her forehead.

"I gotta go," he said. "My dad doesn't like me talking to cops."

"Think about it," she replied. "I'm not blowing smoke, even if I am a cop."

Willy turned around and stopped for a moment. "There are two adults in this world I respect: one is you and the other is your husband," Willy said.

Lucy turned and walked to her house and thought again that she was glad she was learning not to judge. If she had, she would have missed all the gifts she was receiving from Willy.

CHAPTER 29

Just as Bobbie predicted, Colt called Ada the next day to apologize.

"I'm sorry," he said. "I was out of line to leave you like that. I'm glad you made it home safe. It's just that I love you so much I want to be with you and I get frustrated and jealous when you put other things ahead of me. I promise I'll try to understand that you're young and need time to have a life besides your parents. You're just getting away from them and need some time to feel freedom, as long as you promise me that the freedom you want isn't to explore other relationships."

"Trust me, Colt, the last thing I care about right now is a relationship with another man," Ada said with all sincerity.

"What about another woman?" Colt asked.

"Yes, I want relationships with other women, but not the way you're thinking," she replied.

"It's just that you're so beautiful, I don't think you realize how much other men and some women desire you," Colt replied. "You may have one motive for the relationship, but theirs' might be different. You're young and naïve; I'm just looking out for your welfare."

Sure, you are, Ada thought to herself. "I appreciate that," Ada said, trying hard to bite her tongue. "I'm also quite sure that the girls that I'm in a relationship with right now are all straight."

"Why don't you come over and show me how straight you are?" Colt said in a husky voice.

"I hope we can get back to that, but I'm not ready right now," Ada said, throwing cold water on Colt's fire.

"Well you better not wait too long, there're a lot of other girls who want what you have. Not to mention the potential of being rich and famous. Do you know how many NFL quarterbacks are married to models and TV stars?" Colt said, brimming with confidence.

"I wish you all the success in the world, but right now I want to concentrate on being a good volleyball player and a good student," she answered. "After that, I hope to make it in the world on my own merits, and if I get married, I hope my husband will do the same."

"That almost sounds like goodbye," Colt shot back.

"I don't mean it that way, I'm just trying to say right now we're too new in this relationship for me to count on marrying you," Ada replied. "And even if I would be that lucky, I would hope I could still make a contribution to the world besides being Colt Dickson's wife."

Just then Caroline walked in the room and stuck her fingers in her mouth like she was trying to vomit. Ada smiled.

"Colt, I have to go – Caroline just came back and we're going to the library," said Ada.

"You're making a big mistake," he said. "You may get to know Rose after all," and threw his phone down on his bed.

Colt walked to the kitchen, opened the refrigerator and cracked open a beer. Danny was sitting at the table doing one of Colt's papers and looked up in surprise, since Colt rarely drank. Colt held the bottle up to his mouth until it was empty, set it hard onto the counter and said he was going out to clear his head.

Bingo, Danny said to himself, knowing he had his fingerprints. He decided to check out Colt's room to see if he could find any other clues that might help find Rose. He opened the door and immediately saw Colt's phone in the middle of his bed. Just then, a text came through: *Package delivered tonight, stay clear. Delete.*

He didn't know how to open Colt's phone, but he didn't have to. He knew who sent it and what the package was, he just didn't know where it would be delivered.

He pulled out his own cell phone to call Lucy when a hand with lightning speed ripped it from his hand.

Chapter 30

ose was having her usual day sleeping for long segments. Often
somewhere between wake and sleep she would have visions of
her family and what they must be thinking, but more frequently she would
dream of her life over the past year and the turmoil of emotion she would
experience. Those first days at school and the loneliness she felt, yet the
excitement of meeting new friends, being on her own, playing in the band
and attending classes. She re-experienced the excitement of falling in love
for the first time, while also feeling a tug in her gut that told her to be
careful, and the thoughts that this was all moving too fast.

She visualized the sex scenes that were so exciting and taboo, but
sometimes seemed humiliating. The fun of going out for the evening with
her girlfriends, yet the dread of thinking how he would interrogate her the
next day. The joy she felt when her parents would call, and yet the shame
she felt for cutting them off if he was around.

These dreams were often interrupted by her Mexican nurses who
would get her up a couple of times a day to walk. They would walk her
down a short corridor to a small gym to do laps, one on each side of Rose.
The gym reminded her of the high school gym in Keshena where she spent
hours taking shots at the basket from every vantage point on the court. She
remembered the ease at which she moved, the control she had of the ball,
the concentration on the basket as she rose up to shoot. The wonderful
swish the net would make when she made one without hitting the rim.
Now it took all of her effort to stand and put one foot in front of the other.

She was expecting the same routine when her caretakers interrupted her dream. Her doctor was there, giving them directions in Spanish. Soon, for the first time since she could remember, she was outside. The weather was hot and dry – so different from what she had always experienced in Wisconsin. There were few trees but they seemed to be surrounded by mountains that were rocky and smooth at the same time.

CHAPTER 31

Janet Dickson Hughes had done well for herself since she snuck out on Dr. Ron Dickson in the middle of the night, even though her new husband wasn't rich like her former had been…even though she missed her children terribly…even though she still questioned whether she should have put up with the control and abuse so she could have been there for them when they were growing up.

Her life was certainly better. Shortly after leaving she moved in with her sister, and after watching Janet drink and cry for a couple of weeks, her sister gave her the option of living on the streets, going back to Ron –who would probably double the control and abuse – or going to treatment for chemical dependency.

She chose treatment, but it didn't go well in the beginning. She blamed her drinking on her husband, and said she could stop anytime if she could just have her children with her.

"What are the chances of that happening?" her counselor and group members would ask her. Then she would hang her head and cry. Finally, a group member with whom she had become friends took it further.

"What are the chances you'll get your kids back if you're still drinking?" the friend asked.

"None," Janet replied through her tears.

"Well then quit for them," she replied.

"But why does everyone say I have to quit for myself?" Janet questioned.

"Eventually that's true," the counselor said, seeing an inroad, "but that's to stay sober. Let's worry about getting you there in the first place.

For now, use whatever motivation you need to take the first step, which in this case is to admit you are powerless over alcohol and your life has become unmanageable."

From there on Janet took off, even though she never was able to get custody or even visitation with the children. She knew that whatever the case, she wanted them to be proud of what she had become. She had some trouble with the higher power thing, but one day had an insight. Though she didn't believe much in Christ, she did like what he preached. She finally decided it was values like love, forgiveness and especially honesty that would restore her life to sanity. Though she couldn't believe in a deity or religion, she could believe in the values they taught, and they certainly were a power greater than herself, because no matter how hard she tried, she always fell short of completely achieving them.

Now here she was, a safe distance from the Dickson home, sitting in her car with binoculars in hand. It was a spot she knew well, although one she hadn't visited in a while. She would come here often, driving to a hill overlooking the house when the kids were growing up and watching them play in the yard. It took all the skills she had learned in treatment, all the mantras, like *one day at a time, easy does it, do the next right thing*, to keep from drinking after Danny had his accident. It broke her heart to watch him play catch with Colt while he was sitting in his wheelchair. The things that used to come so easy for him now were a struggle, but she learned from him as she watched him not get discouraged and not give up. She saw him slowly gain skill with his wheelchair.

Now here she was again, sitting in this familiar spot and watching the Dickson house, but for what? What was she even supposed to look for?

She scanned the house and yard and saw nothing out of the ordinary. Then she moved the binoculars toward the guest house and noticed one of the windows had its shades drawn. Ron hated company and those rooms were never used. She watched the house for a while and eventually saw a woman in a nurse's outfit leave the building and soon return. Even stranger, at one point, she saw Ron go in wearing his surgical mask. She tried calling Danny, but got no answer.

A little while later, she watched as Ron came back out of the guesthouse, this time pushing a wheelchair with a young woman sitting slumped over. A dark-haired man and woman help him get the young woman in the front seat of the airplane. Then they climbed in back and took off down the runway. At the end, Ron turned the plane around, roared the engines and soon they were flying above the hills that surrounded the Dickson home.

She tried calling Danny once more but only got his voicemail. She decided not to leave a message in case his brother might retrieve it instead. Little did she know it was his brother who was holding Danny's phone.

Janet ended the call just as flashing red lights appeared in her rear-view mirror. Sherriff Chris Stanfield stepped out of his patrol car and Janet knew immediately she was in trouble. She had met the sheriff before, and had called him more than once after she and Ron had been fighting, but it was always Janet on whom the sheriff had focused his attention.

Now Janet, have you been drinking again? he would ask.

But Chris, he hit me, she would counter.

Where? I don't see any marks.

He hits me in the stomach. There'll be a bruise tomorrow.

Well I think you need to stop drinking so much and running into things. So, doc, do we still have a 10 a.m. tee time tomorrow?

Sure do, Ron would say. *Let me walk you to the door.*

Then they would walk out, talking in hushed tones. After a while Janet didn't bother calling anymore.

"Janet, you know Ron has a restraining order against you," he said as he approached the car.

"Yes, how ironic is that?" she replied.

"Well you have no business out here spying on him," he answered.

"I don't suppose you'd believe me if I told you he's been holding a young woman captive in his guest house and now he's flown off with her somewhere?" she replied.

"Janet, are you back on the sauce?" he sneered.

"No, but I see you're still in my ex-husband's pocket," she replied.

She could tell that got to him as his expression stiffened.

"Well speaking of your ex, he believes it's time to teach you to stop spying on him," he said. "You'll have to come with me."

CHAPTER 32

When Ron Dickson landed at the airport, Cindy wasn't working, and the Launching Pad was slammed with customers. By the time Cindy called Lucy, Cindy guessed at least an hour had passed. The sun was just nibbling on the trees that were beginning to turn color on the horizon. Lucy realized that Lieutenant Moon's plan wasn't going to work. Dickson would already be long gone from Shawano and on his way to the drug dealer's farmhouse just inside Brown County.

She and Ray agreed there was no time for consulting with superiors, but they did call Agent Scruggs and left a message. They knew they would both be out of jobs and maybe in jail if they were wrong. Ray grabbed his rifle and his ghillie suit a camo suit he kept from his sniper days and Lucy her Glock as they headed for their squad. They were at least 20 miles away, but Lucy turned on the dome lights and they screamed up Highway 29, turning onto a county road just before Maple Wood Meats.

It was completely dark now and they were close to the farmhouse. Lucy shut off the dome lights and even her headlights. They decided to take a run by first before setting up their plan. The plan took a quick turn when they got to where it used to be and discovered the house had been leveled.

For a while Ray and Lucy sat silently. They were frustrated, and both were thinking of their next move. Luckily, shortly after they arrived at the empty lot, Scruggs called. He informed them that the FBI had the house leveled shortly after Kane and his friends went to prison.

"What are you doing next?" Scruggs asked.

"I think we'll both pray," Lucy said.

CHAPTER 33

"Since you're so worried about Rose, dear brother, let me take you to see her," Colt sneered as he held a handgun to Danny's neck and pushed him from his bedroom toward the front door.

"I didn't know you owned a gun," Danny said to Colt before they reached the front door.

"You're about to find out about a lot of things I wish you didn't know," Colt replied. "I want you to know I regret all of it."

Danny believed he was sincere.

As Colt push Danny toward his car, Matt came walking up the sidewalk.

"Where you guys off to?" he asked.

"It's a family matter," Colt said quickly, not stopping to talk. Then Colt opened the door for his brother and assisted him into his handicap-accessible van. Danny used his hands to slide from his wheelchair to the front seat of the van. Then Colt buckled him into the driver's seat and pushed the wheelchair up the ramp into the back before climbing into the passenger side.

"Not to worry, buddy, I'm just having a slight physical problem like I had at the gym the other night," he said to Matt, closing the driver's door. "Colt's taking me for a follow-up visit."

Colt closed the door on the passenger side. "That was smart, brother," Colt said as they sped off.

"I thought so," Danny said.

Matt was halfway up the walk to the townhouse when he realized what Danny was saying. Luckily the Bolt brothers were pulling up just as it hit him. He jumped in the car. "Follow Colt and Danny," he said, "but don't let him see you."

Thinking he was joking, Eli started to bring the car to a stop. "I think Colt's taking Danny to Rose and they both might end up dead." The sound of Matt's voice told Eli to do as he was asked.

Once Eli was following at a safe distance, Matt got out his phone and called Ada.

Ada was down the hall visiting Rachel and her phone lay unanswered on her bed. Caroline picked it up just before it went to voicemail.

"Yo," she said.

"Ada?" Matt said, sounding confused.

"No, Ada's down the hall, it's Caroline," she replied.

"Caroline, we need Bobbie to get a hold of Lucy right away," Danny instructed. "Colt has Danny in the car and we think he's taking him to Rose. After what happened the other night, I don't think Danny will be coming back, and if Rose is still alive, I don't think she will be for long."

Caroline listened as she walked down the hall to Bobbie's room. As soon as Bobbie answered the door, Caroline gave her the phone. "I think we got the son of a bitch, or in this case, the son of a bastard," she said.

Matt quickly explained the situation to Bobbie. "Where are you?" she asked. "Are you heading toward a farmhouse?"

Matt paused for a moment, not sure what that meant. "I think we might be – we just passed the stadium and seem to be heading out of town," replied.

"The stadium?" Bobbie questioned. "That would be in the wrong direction."

Bobbie handed the phone to Caroline and used her own phone to call Lucy. When she reached her, Lucy was sitting in her squad with Ray, and both were just staring into space wondering what they could possibly do next. When Bobbie told her what Matt had said, her eyes lit up. She looked to heaven silently and mouthed *Thank you.*

She sped off with no explanation to Ray, but she knew he would understand with what she said next.

"You need to tell those boys to make sure they hang way back, especially when they reach the country. When the van stops, stay at least several blocks from where they are. If there's a side road, pull into it and shut off the lights. Tell them to stay on the phone and describe their position. We'll be there as soon as we can." Lucy flicked on her lights to get through Green Bay as soon as possible.

On the way, she explained to Ray as much as she could from her most recent dream.

"I think what's going to happen is they're going to make a porn movie with Rose," she said. "I don't know much about it, but I bet it will start with her reading a newspaper or watching the news. That's important because the film needs to have proof of a date on it. I will bet they will have Danny playing some role in the film too, maybe even holding a gun on her. That way they can implicate him in Rose's disappearance in the first place. After the film, they can do an overdose or maybe a murder-suicide."

While continuing to talk and give directions, the girls assembled in Rachel's room. Rachel and Ada soon caught up on what was happening. In the long pauses, Caroline convinced them that they may be able to help in some way and they piled in Bobbie's car.

When they were out of Green Bay near St. Norman's football stadium, Lucy shut off her dome lights and slowed down. As they approached the location where they expected the Bolts and Matt to be, she shut off her headlights. A block before they reached the intersection where they could make out the outline of the Bolts' car, Lucy slowed her squad to a slow roll and Ray got out. He carried his rifle and made his way to the house through the tall golden cornstalks that within days from now would be harvested.

As he ran he began to have flashbacks of Africa, where he chased the men and boys who raped and murdered the villagers where he stayed. *This is not Africa, this is Wisconsin. Focus on the moment, where am I placing my feet, how am I breathing, how are my hands clasping the rifle.*

When Ray came to the back of the house, he found a window with a light shining through. Ray could see Rose sitting on a couch wearing a negligee and watching the news on TV. It was probably a recording, but the events would be things that had happened since her disappearance. Ray could see Danny sitting in his chair and holding a gun, but he was also nodding off, so Ray guessed Danny was experiencing heroin for the first time. He could also see another man behind him off camera holding a gun on both of them.

Now Ray wished he could be in a different moment. He decided on the sequence of his shots. The night was calm and because of the corn he used for cover, he had a relatively close shot, so he knew he wouldn't miss. He had to take out the man with the gun first, and hoped he could just disable him, but with two people in his line of fire, he decided he couldn't risk it.

He called Lucy and described the situation.

"I'm going to turn on my siren and go in through the front," she said. "Does the man with the gun look ready to fire?"

"No, he looks kind of bored," Ray answered.

"Good, if he raises his gun, you'll have to disable him as best you can. I'm hoping he'll run when he hears the siren," she replied.

With that, she turned on her siren and soon was at the front door. She pounded with her gun and yelled "Police! Open up!"

Ray watched as the man with the gun looked toward the front and with that, Ray fired his weapon. The first shot shattered the window and hit the door frame right next to the gunman's ear and sent wood flying – some of which punctured the side of his face. With that, he dropped his gun and ran through the door. Ray's second shot went through the camera and he watched the cameraman fall to the ground, and the third hit the television. He then saw Rose move as in a daze and sit on Danny's lap. Danny, now awake, wheeled his chair out of sight.

Then Ray moved quickly and silently to a new vantage point in the front of the house where it looked like a fire drill gone wrong was taking place. There were people in various stages of undress, and many staggering from drugs and alcohol, streaming out the door into the cool night air.

When the front door flew open, Lucy fell to the ground. When she recovered, Lucy – Glock in hand – told everyone to freeze, but caught between panic and intoxication, most continued to run.

Eli Bolt had followed Lucy and pulled up behind her patrol car. Lucy ordered them to stay in the car and "Video the events on their phones, you will be witnesses." Lucy fired her gun in the air and most of the panicked fell to the ground, where they seemed to stay put. Those that didn't made the mistake of running toward the cornfield where Ray was waiting. The boys did as they were told and observed but seemed to concentrate mostly on the half-naked women.

Just as order was beginning to be restored, shots rang out from inside the house and the first shot sent tree bark flying about a foot away from the patrol car. The three boys ducked below the windows of their car, digging in as deeply as they could. Two shots came from the cornfield where Ray had positioned himself. With that, the shots from inside the house ceased and two of the men Lucy recognized from the car that had stopped Bobbie on the Rez came out with their hands up.

"How many are left inside?" Lucy asked with gun pointed at the first man's head.

"I don't know," he answered. "What right do you have to do this? We run a legitimate business here."

"I'm sure part of it is, but you're under arrest for the rest of it," Lucy answered, then yelled toward Ray. "Ray, if they try to run, shoot them. I'm going in."

Lucy ran toward the front steps and though they couldn't see Ray hiding in the corn, the men knew he was out there and didn't move. She entered the front door with her gun drawn and holding it with both hands. The house was dark and it took a moment for her eyes to adjust. She jerked her body left and right, not being sure exactly what she was looking for other than someone aiming a gun at her.

Her eyes landed a on a dim light in the bathroom and someone pouring a substance in the toilet. She fired her gun at the handle of the toilet, blowing metal from porcelain before he could flush it. The man came out of the bathroom with his hands in the air. He walked toward her and she could see it was the man who had kept his back to her while threatening Bobbie. She knew now she had seen him in the old farmhouse with Kane, and he was one of the men in Willy's sketches.

"Go join your buddies in front of the house," she ordered. "Where's Dickson?"

The man walked by her without speaking.

Lucy continued further into the house, turning in each direction through each doorway, when she reached the room where the filming had been taking place. She found Rose alive, still sitting on Danny's lap with her head on his shoulder. Danny was staring straight ahead, still under the influence of the drugs he'd been given. Behind him were Colt and Ron Dickson, both with guns pointed at Rose and Danny.

"Drop your gun, or they die," Ron Dickson said coldly.

"Aren't they going to die anyway?" Lucy asked.

"Give me some credit," Dickson said. "Even I know this game is over. I'm a healer, not a killer, whether you believe that or not. I just want to get Colt and me safely out of the country. Let us leave and I'll leave Danny and Rose at the airport. Drop your gun or this will end badly for all of us."

Lucy placed her gun on the floor and raised her hands. "I don't want anyone hurt."

Outside Ray had left his position in front of the house and moved through the corn to his original position in back where he could see Lucy drop her gun and Colt quickly pick it up. Then she watched as Lucy lead them back through the door. He saw Colt had a gun in his hand, but instead of pointing it at Danny, he was holding the gun and the handles of Danny's wheelchair, trying to maneuver around in the shattered doorway. Ray moved back to the front of the house and toward the car where the boys were still hunkered down.

"Hey, kid, you have a football in that car?" he whispered.

"Yes," Ethan said, still afraid to look up.

"Can you throw that thing or just catch it?" Ray asked.

"I was a quarterback in high school," Ethan replied.

"Good, in a few moments, Colt will be coming out with a gun. When I say 'now,' you throw the ball at Colt's gun. Then get out of the way," Ray instructed.

A few moments later, Lucy walked out of the front door with her hands raised, but the rest did not follow.

"Tell the guy in the cornfield to drop his gun and come out with his hands raised," Dickson instructed.

"No," Lucy said firmly.

"Do it or I'll put a bullet in the back of your head."

"Then you and Colt will be dead for sure," she replied.

With that, Danny, gradually recovering from the heroin, pushed on his wheels as hard as he could, knocking Lucy from the porch and pulling Colt out the door.

"Now!" Ray yelled, and Ethan fired a bullet pass that hit Colt in his gun hand, then squarely in his face. Colt's gun fired once toward the ground. With Rose still in his lap, Danny pulled Colt with him and they all fell at the bottom of the steps. Ron Dickson came out firing wildly before Ray shot him in his gun hand, the bullet ricocheting into his leg and sending him to the ground.

Bobbie and the girls pulled up just as all this was happening and were able to be additional witnesses.

Lucy pulled herself from the ground and retrieved her gun and Ron Dickson's weapon. She then called the Green Bay police and an ambulance. Once they arrived, she showed them the heroin from the house as well as large amounts of cash. They took away Alex and his band and the ambulance took Ron Dickson and two other wounded men.

The boys agreed to take Danny to Maehnowesekiyah, and the girls would take Rose. Lucy and Ray would take Colt to the Tribal police jail where Scruggs could officially arrest him. Lucy at first felt relieved that she and Ray had survived, but for the first time, she realized the real danger still lurked ahead: Lieutenant Moon.

CHAPTER 34

Lucy was right to be afraid. She had never seen Lieutenant Moon that mad before. He was particularly mad at Ray.

"This is the second time you've gone off on your own and people end up shot!" he said with a booming voice.

"Please, sir," Ray started.

"I don't want to hear about PTSD or the fact that you saved a little boy, or in this case Rose Waukau. The Police department is like the military. No one should know that better than you. You have to follow the chain of command and unless you got a promotion that I don't know about, you are under my chain of command. Do you think you could have at least notified me of what you were doing?" he asked.

"Sir, we thought about that," Lucy tried to interrupt. "But we knew what kind of a bind that would have put you in."

"Oh! So, you were just being considerate of my feelings. Is that right, sweet Lucy?" he countered.

"Well, yes, sir," Lucy replied quietly.

"Do you think this is some sort of touchy-feely welfare organization we're running here?" he continued.

"No, sir," Lucy and Ray both mumbled.

"That's good, because let me show you what kind of an organization this is. You two are both suspended until…"

Just then the door opened and an embarrassed secretary apologized, "I'm sorry, I tried to tell them they had to wait, but they said they'd been doing nothing but that for months now and couldn't wait any longer."

Lieutenant Moon's voice did a one-eighty.

"Mr. and Mrs. Waukau," he said gently.

Neither of the Waukaus seemed to pay much attention to the lieutenant. Both were crying, both ran to Lucy and Ray, who hugged them and rocked them as the tears freely flowed from all of them. Through sobs they kept taking turns talking.

"We were just about to give up all hope of ever finding her alive, but you two never quit," Mrs. Waukau sobbed.

"We hear even your own children were threatened," Mr. Waukau said with tears dripping on Ray's shoulders. "Yet you kept on and saved our baby."

"You risked your own lives, and saved her from terrible indignity that would had been filmed and seen by every creep imaginable," Mrs. Waukau blurted out just as another wave of sobs started.

"We just met that band of kids who helped you invade that terrible house," said Mr. Waukau. "They told us the whole story."

Lieutenant Moon's eyes widened.

"Oh! We hadn't gotten to that point in our debriefing," he said. "You enlisted children to help you infiltrate a drug house?" The lieutenant's voice now a mixture of kindness and sarcasm only Lucy and Ray would catch.

"Well, sir, they were college students actually, and they really do deserve a lot of credit for helping us to crack this case," Lucy said. "We hope you'll consider some sort of ceremony to honor them," Lucy said, enjoying the pickle in which the lieutenant now found himself.

"How is your daughter doing?" said the lieutenant, quickly managing to change the subject.

Their faces changed from joy to fear and concern. Mr. Waukau spoke first.

"Well, she's alive and we hope she'll make a full recovery, but there are a number of concerns at this point," he said. "First, there's a question of brain damage. It may sound strange, but thank God a brain surgeon kidnapped her. It appears he did all the right things to keep her alive and help her heal."

"Then there's the question of the drugs," Mrs. Waukau added. "There's no doubt she's addicted to heroin and will need detox and probably treatment. But we'll deal with those issues as they happen. Right now, we're just thankful to Lucy and Ray and those wonderful kids that she's alive."

The waterworks started again. Lieutenant Moon put his hand on Mrs. Waukau's back and in a very subtle way, moved her toward the door.

"That certainly is good news, and we're all grateful to Ray and Lucy," Lieutenant Moon said, hoping the Waukaus didn't notice his lack of enthusiasm. "We need to debrief a little more, and then I'll send them over to the treatment center to join you with your daughter."

With one more round of hugs, the Waukaus left. As soon as the door closed, the growl started. It was almost inaudible at first, but it started deep in the lieutenant's ample belly and grew louder as he stared at Lucy and Ray. After a while, the growl was mixed with words that seem to make the lieutenant choke.

"Okay, I'm changing your suspension to a desk assignment, but first I want to know every detail of what happened, and why you decided you needed to do this on your own," he said. "Then you're going to work day and night putting together a case against these people, because it's not just their lives on the line, it's your jobs as well. And Ray, for the second time, you could be facing jail yourself."

The three of them sat down and Lucy and Ray gave him every detail they could remember. Moon spoke a little, but he didn't have to. His expressions ranged from rolling his eyes at some of the smaller details, to covering his face with his hands, and finally dropping his head to his desk and growling again.

When Ray and Lucy finally left his office, they simply looked at each other and first took a deep breath with a very long exhale and then just a hint of a smile.

CHAPTER 35

Rose gradually recovered physically, but her mental, emotional and spiritual recovery was slower. She stayed at Maehnowesekiyah for over a month, and her parents brought in specialists to assess her brain activity, which, as near as anyone was able to determine, had returned to normal.

At first, she had a hard time accepting the 12 Steps. They found that her captors had not only given her heroin, but during the time of the attempted film, she was given Rohypnol – sometimes called roofies or the date rape drug on the street – to keep her from remembering what happened to her.

"I'm not even 21," she would say during group treatment. "I've never had a legal drink and now you tell me I should give up all mind-altering drugs. It's not fair; I didn't choose this."

They would reply: *So, go back out there and use by choice, and come back in here years from now after your looks are destroyed and your life is in shambles. Maybe you can have a couple of kids by various men that get taken from you. This may be an opportunity for you to bypass all that and make a life for yourself. Besides, what kind of a choice do you think some kid born to two alcoholic or drug-addicted parents has of not becoming addicted themselves and needing to do exactly what you are doing?*

Eventually, with the patience of Dr. Wolf who took a special interest in her, and Lucy, who she chose as her sponsor, Rose came around. She began to say, "I may not have chosen to use drugs, but I am sure going to choose **not** use them."

She worked through the steps in time and began to enjoy going to meetings and helping other women with their issues. She became particularly interested in their relationships with men and deciding for herself, what was a healthy relationship and what was not. Luckily, she also had her parents' relationship as a healthy model.

She also used the sweat lodge to help her heal. Though the heat was sometimes nearly unbearable, she enjoyed sweating and purging her body of the evil she was surrounded by for several months. She liked leaving some of her problems with the grandfathers, who were the rocks that were heated in fire for hours before the sweat and were added to those rocks already in the lodge with each additional round. She began to see the spirits like tiny points of light that seemed to be attending to her and her friends in the lodge. Little by little, she was able to remember what had happened to her and help Lucy and Ray put together a case against Colt and his father.

She remembered the night leaving work and driving home from her neighbors' house. When she arrived home, Colt was waiting for her in the driveway. When she got out of her car, she told Colt that she was tired and not interested in talking to him.

Listen, you dumb Indian, you don't blow me off like that after I drove all the way out here just to talk with you, he had said.

Watch me, she replied, and continued walking into her house.

"That's the last thing I remember, until I woke up what I would guess was a couple of weeks later in what I was told was a hospital," she said. "I think they probably kept me in a coma on purpose to allow the swelling in my brain to subside. I was still pretty dazed and confused and for quite a few more days, I just stayed in bed and tried to make sense of what was happening to me.

"My doctor, who I believe now was Colt's father, would come and see me but I began to think it was strange that he was always wearing a surgical mask. When I asked him, he said he had just come out of surgery and didn't want to infect me with anything that might slow down my progress. I told him his voice sounded familiar and I asked if I knew him. He told me it was probably from hearing him speak while I was in a coma.

"After a while, they stopped giving me shots and started giving me pain pills, when I said my head didn't hurt anymore. The nurse told me it was to keep the swelling down. Dr. Wolf told me it was probably Oxycontin. Then I started pretending to swallow the pills but would spit them out when no one was looking. I would get out of bed at night when the nurse would leave the room and look out the window. Once I was caught, it was back to the injections, and I was pretty out of it until I found myself here. I don't remember anything about flying anywhere, but I know when I looked out the window, I wasn't anywhere around here."

Thanks to Lieutenant Moon's suggestion, they were able to compare prints on the car and prints on the gun Colt was holding at the farmhouse and found a match. That put Colt with Rose after they supposedly broke up. Colt's roommates said Colt had gone to his room early and they thought he was just resting up for the double-day football practices, but he could have easily left without them noticing.

CHAPTER 36

W hen they interrogated Colt and Ron Dickson, they also included Agent Scruggs from the FBI since there was evidence that Dr. Dickson had transported Rose across numerous state lines. At first, neither would talk about what had happened to Rose, and Dr. Dickson soon brought in a team of lawyers who began to talk with the D.A. about a plea bargain.

The D.A. agreed to a lighter sentence in exchange for the truth about what had happened to Rose and for information about the drug dealers who had threatened Bobbie, Lucy and Ray's family, and helped them hatch a plan that would exonerate them from any responsibility in Rose's disappearance.

Once they had some of the charges dropped against them, first Colt described what happened the night Rose disappeared. He had left the townhouse without alerting his roommates, because he didn't want to get teased about stalking a girl who was no longer interested in him. His plan was only to talk with Rose about rekindling their relationship and to promise her he would change. He was mad when she refused to even talk with him, and when she walked by him, he pushed her so that she hit her head on the car and was knocked unconscious. She was bleeding and wouldn't respond when he shook her and called her name.

"I panicked and called my dad, who luckily had not left for home yet," he said. "He came the 12 miles from Shawano to Rose's house and told me he'd take care of it and I should leave. I knew if anyone could help her, he could, and I left. I drove around for a while til I knew all my roommates would be asleep and I snuck back into the townhouse. I didn't sleep much that night, and the next morning, I called my dad and asked him if Rose was okay. He told me I should concentrate on football and not worry about Rose.

"'Dad,' I said, "'you've got to tell me something or I'll never be able to let it go. Is she dead?'"

"He said she was alive and would make a full recovery, and he was working on a plan so that he could return her without her being able to implicate me in what happened."

"I'm curious why – when you had an ex who was fighting for her life because of you -- still started a new relationship with Ada and ended up with the same set of problems all over again?" Lucy asked.

"Now wait a minute," Colt said, "a big part of what happened was Rose's fault. If she had just talked to me like I asked and agreed to go back to the way things were, none of this would have happened. My dad was mad at me at first for getting involved with Ada, but even he agreed that it was better that I move on, and it made it look more normal anyway. Besides, how would I know that Ada would end up being the same kind of nut case as Rose?"

"A Rose by any other name," Ray mumbled.

"What's that?" Colt wondered out loud, having skipped most of English Lit.

"Oh, nothing, just quoting Shakespeare," Ray replied.

"So, what made you force your brother into the situation with Rose?" Ray asked.

"I think he was more in love with Rose than I was," Colt said. "He just couldn't let it go and he was turning against his own family. What else could I do?"

Next, they interrogated Ron Dickson. Later, Lucy, Ray and Agent Scruggs all commented about the similarity between father and son.

"What could I do?" he asked. "I was caught between protecting my son and saving that girl's life. I knew if I just dropped her off at the emergency room in Shawano, she would probably die, or have serious brain damage. I'm not just a neurosurgeon – I specialize in treating brain trauma. I knew she was better off in my hands. I had no choice but to take her back with me to Texas. I not only kept her in a coma to keep the swelling down, I had to operate to stop a brain bleed. That girl can thank me for the fact that she'll be able to live a normal life, and even complete college if she wants to do that."

"What about the fact that you purposely addicted her to heroin and possibly set her up to overdose after she acted in that movie?" they asked.

"I had to protect my son, and besides the movie and what happened afterward was strictly up to those thugs in Green Bay," Dickson replied.

"Which leads me to another question," Agent Scruggs continued. "How does a neurosurgeon from Texas hook up with some low-life drug pushers from Wisconsin?"

This is the question for which Dr. Dickson had been waiting. He was hoping it was his get- out-of-jail-free card. He turned to his lawyer, who gave him a nod. As it turned out, Dr. Dickson and Sheriff Stanfield were more that golfing buddies. For a long time, the sheriff had been on the payroll of a Mexican drug cartel, and Ron Dickson had gradually given into the huge amounts of cash waved his way. He would allow them to use his airstrip for deliveries. He set up his guesthouse with operating and recovery rooms for the occasional times that some of the cartel members were hurt in gun battles with police or rival cartels. In return, he not only received lots of money, but even a professional staff to man the hospital – all paid for by the cartel. Since most of the staff was in the country illegally, there was very little chance they would go to the authorities with information about what went on at the guesthouse/hospital.

Janet Hughes was just being released from jail when the FBI agents came in and arrested the sheriff. She had been held much longer than she should have been, but the sheriff, up until that moment, didn't worry about technicalities.

The sheriff turned to Janet.

"That SOB ex-husband of yours screwed me to save his own skin," he said.

"Gee sheriff, I don't see any marks," she replied. "You would have to pull down your pants and let me have a look. Are you sure you haven't been drinking again and just imagined all this?"

Janet turned to the FBI agents and told them she had seen Dr. Dickson leaving his guesthouse pushing someone in a wheelchair. She said that the person was covered in a sheet but she was quite sure that it was the missing girl from Wisconsin. She told them she would be glad to testify as to what she had seen. They asked her to fly up to Green Bay for a grand jury that had recently been formed by the prosecutor.

As she left the police station, Janet thought that she had worked really hard to let go of the resentments she had of her husband and the sheriff. She could tell over the years that she had made progress, but knew as she was thinking about seeing her boys and no longer trapped by her ex-husband and his friends that she was now truly free of that debilitating pain of resentment.

Her current husband, Rick, looked at her quizzically as she jumped in the air and raised her arms as she walked to the car. Rick was a retired schoolteacher and they had been married for 15 years. He was also in recovery from alcohol. She opened the door and slid into the car beside him, giving him a big hug and a long, hard kiss.

"I'm going to see if I can't arrange to have you locked up at least once a week," he said with a smile.

"How would you like to take a second honeymoon with me to beautiful Green Bay, Wisconsin?" she asked. "I think there may still be some fall colors up there, and maybe we could take in a Packer game and get some cherries in Door County."

"After that last kiss, I'd follow you anywhere, but you have to promise me to take a shower first," he laughed. "You smell a little gamey."

Janet smiled. "I wasn't about to shower in that jail with that sheriff lurking around," she replied. "I'm sure they have cameras or peepholes in the shower. But that's part of my joy – that creep is going to jail. But a better part is so is the good – and I use that term loosely – Dr. Dickson. The best part, though, is that I get to see my boys, even though one will be in jail."

Janet and Rick flew to Green Bay and Janet met first with Danny. Rick stayed back at the hotel while Janet and Danny met for lunch. They talked for hours and then Danny took her to the townhouse to meet his roommates. She immediately liked them all, and Rick came over and met them as well.

Janet's meeting with Colt was not quite as joyful. It was hard to have to talk with him on a phone separated by a glass wall. It was even more difficult seeing him in an orange jumpsuit with numbers on the back, knowing what that would mean for him. She tried to think back to her own worst moments and how, in the long run, they often lead to her recovery and where she was now.

She had been studying mindfulness, which was recommended by her sponsor, and one of the best lessons she had learned was that nothing – not drugs, not alcohol – could make pleasure last forever, and that pain is also always changing, and most of the time, doesn't last forever either.

At first, Colt was cold and distant with her. He told her how much he hated her for leaving. He asked about some of the things his father had told him about her, and she answered as honestly as she could. They had just started making progress when their time together was up, but the next day she was back, and the day after that as well.

On the fourth day, she noticed he smiled when he saw her. She would be leaving to return to Texas the next day, and wouldn't be back, she told him, and some of the distance returned.

"I would like very much to stay in touch with you, no matter what happens at the trial and beyond," she said. "If you're willing, I'd like to call and write. I'll come back up for the trial, and if you need a place to stay when you get out of jail, you're welcome with us."

For the first time, she saw a tear in his eye. "I would like that," he said.

CHAPTER 37

After Rose got out of treatment, she decided to visit St. Norman's for a weekend. She wanted to see how she would react seeing the people and places she had become so familiar with the year before. She stayed with Rachel, whose roommate had dropped out after getting several failing notices at midterm. She visited the girls she had gotten to know the previous year, and all said how very glad they were to see her, but she found herself spending most of her time with Bobbie, Ada, Caroline and Rachel. They went to one of the last football games and though he didn't quite have Colt's skills, Ethan had become the quarterback and did a good job filling in for him. It was hard to replace Ethan as receiver, but Ethan and Eli had incredible chemistry. It seemed that whenever Eli turned to look for the ball, there it was.

The next day, Rose asked if the girls would all go to mass with her. They all agreed, but Caroline was convinced the roof would collapse the moment she walked into the sanctuary. Rose had gotten to be good friends with a priest named Fr. Mack, a red-haired Irishman full of stories about his family back home.

Even though he was a monk at the abbey at St. Norman's, he had spent some time at the parish in Keshena because of the shortage of priests in the Green Bay diocese. Rose played the guitar at mass and accompanied his beautiful Irish tenor voice. Because Fr. Mack was used to living in a community of monks, he felt lonely being all alone in the rectory at St. David's in Keshena, so he often had dinner with the Waukaus where he had a standing invitation.

They got to be friends, and part of the reason Rose decided to attend St. Norman's was because he had returned to the abbey after having a series of health problems. He had been the only one she had confided in when she and Colt started having problems.

When Fr. Mack walked down the aisle of the church and saw the beautiful young women lined up in the first pew with Rose in the middle, he smiled and wiped a tear from his eye.

When it came to the sermon of the mass, he first acknowledged Rose and again began to tear up when he said he had been preparing himself for the day her parents would ask him to say her funeral mass.

"I would have said yes," he said, "but it would have been like saying a mass for one of my family members, and we are all old codgers now. Saying that mass for you, losing you in the prime of your life with such huge potential, well, that may have been the hardest thing I would ever have to do. But here you are and so this is not about death but about life, and today we celebrate you, but not just you: let's all of us celebrate today that we are alive and none of us should take that for granted. We need all to live as though today may be our last day on earth, so let's make the most of it."

He continued: "Now even if you're not into the bible, you may want to pay attention to Corinthians 13, which was our epistle for today. Many of you are experiencing what we call romantic love for the first time and are wondering if it is something that you can build into a life-long relationship. Well, I'm here to tell you, the answer is no. Scott Peck says romantic love is lust, while true love is always effort or risk. Bishop Sheen says love is not an emotion – it is an act of the will. If it was an emotion, God couldn't command you to love your neighbor. What some of you are experiencing is attraction, and in some cases, that is a bad thing, since who you are attracted to is not what you need.

"Some of you have already experienced the fact that you keep being attracted to someone who leaves you feeling the way your father or mother made you feel. If you have an alcoholic father, you may be attracted to alcoholics. But what does this have to do with St. Paul's epistle? Well, St. Paul tells us not only what love is, but also what it is not. He says love is patient, kind, protective, hopeful, trusting, true and slow to anger. He says love isn't envious, self-seeking, boastful, proud – and I might add, controlling and critical. He says love does not keep score. Now, as some of you know, each week at the end of mass, I ask about birthdays and anniversaries, so I know there are many of you out there who have been married for 20 years and more. How many of you have love exactly like this all the time? Let's see a show of hands. Let the record show no hands were raised," Fr. Mack said in his best lawyer imitation to laughs from the congregation.

"None of us are perfect, but this is a standard by which you can judge your relationships. If you are in pain most of the time, if you are experiencing the negatives of St. Paul's list much more than the positives, then maybe you don't have a relationship that is worth building a life around. Pain will find you often enough, but you don't have to invite it into your life."

At the end of mass, Fr. Mack said, "Go now and live love as it is meant to be. Pope Francis says whenever we encounter another in love, we learn something new about God."

CHAPTER 38

The following semester, Rose returned to St. Norman's. She moved in with Rachael, and the two of them and hung out with Ada, Caroline and Bobbie. Ada and Rose had no interest in getting into another serious relationship, Bobbie was still waiting for Austin to return from Afghanistan, and Rachael and Caroline dated occasionally, but not seriously. However, all of them hung out a lot with Danny, Matt, Eli and Ethan. Their friendship grew and all believed they'd stay friends forever.

Ada continued with volleyball, and Rose continued in band. The next year, they all returned to school. Ada stuck to her word and took studying seriously. She had fun, but also worked hard physically and mentally.

Because of the plea agreement, Colt did not have to stand trial, but he did end up with a jail sentence, as did his father. Janice returned to Green Bay and visited both Danny and Colt. Colt was able to finish his degree in prison and took advantage of a men's group while there that focused on domestic violence. After he was released, he took up his mother's offer to live with her and Rick. He got a chance to see what a healthy relationship was like and became close to his stepdad. He, too, focused on friendships with women.

Lucy and Ray got reassigned to their regular duties and had a long investigation by the review board. They delighted in their children and family and did their jobs as best they could. Ray continued at times to struggle with PTSD, but with the help of his family, he continued to heal.

Lucy, true to her word, took Willy to the College of Menominee Nation and enrolled him in art classes. Soon after, she had an encounter with Willy's father, who slurred, "Why are you filling my son with silly notions?"

Just then, Ray showed up and pulled Willy's dad aside. He never told Lucy what he said to him, but they were never called to Willy's house again for domestic problems.

TEXT AND ACKNOWLEDGEMENTS

M any people who read this book and are familiar with the Green Bay area might immediately think to themselves, *Hey, that's St. Norbert's he's writing about, not St. Norman's.* Well, that's the setting I chose, and though St. Norbert's doesn't have a Lombardi Hall, the Green Bay Packers do hold their summer camp there on the Fox River, and one of my favorite bike trails is right across the river. I changed the name because though I wanted a college setting, I didn't want abuse to be associated with any one particular college. This is a problem that is universal. It exists in all cultures, all economic classes, all religions, and all professions, and all sexual orientations.

One thing I wanted to make clear is that it is not a problem that exists only in marital relationships, and I wrote this book to help eventual victims to recognize some of the symptoms that occur, some of which do not appear to be that of an abuser.

Abuse is often cyclical. It can start with a ***romantic phase*** that may last for a long time. Here economics may play a part, but might include flowers and candy, as well as lavish dates, compliments, poetry or jewelry. It's important to point out here that this does not mean that all people who do this will end up as abusers, but there may be other warning signs during this phase. Notice that Colt had difficulty taking responsibility for anything. An incomplete pass was the receiver's fault.

Let's call the next phase the ***control phase***. Here the compliments might shift a little. "I liked your last hairstyle better," or "The dress you had on last week was more your color" or "You used to have an incredible figure."

These are designed consciously or unconsciously to begin to erode the victim's confidence.

Other control issues may also be shrouded in praise and love. "I don't want you to ever have to work, I want to take care of you." This can sound appealing, especially to a woman who has always dreamed of having children and having a husband who made enough money to allow her to stay home and take care for them.

A third issue that may seem romantic in the beginning is the boyfriend who wants to spend all his time with his girlfriend and acts jealous not only of other guys, but even of her girlfriends and family members. The end result of all this can be a victim who, after experiencing abuse, may want to leave, but at this point, has lost her self-confidence, has no means of supporting herself, and has little or no emotional support system. Now let's add to this the cycle that abuse may follow.

Let's start again with the **honeymoon phase** followed by increased criticism, control, and also setting high expectations for the victim that she eventually falls short of, leading to abuse. The victim now may threaten to leave, but again, has nowhere to turn. She may tell herself she will leave in the morning, and after a restless night, may even pack a bag (obviously having children will complicate this further).

At this point the abuser may be filled with remorse, perhaps even sincere. He may apologize for the abuse, often adding, "But you make me crazy when you don't have dinner ready when I get home," or "I can't stand it when I catch you looking at other men. Not to mention, my boss is driving me crazy, too."

He then may promise that it will never happen again, and that will be followed by a honeymoon phase including the flowers, etc. By the time the abuse happens again, the victim is more convinced they are worthless and lucky to have the relationship they have. They have invested more time and energy, and may have additional dependents. The abuser may add additional baggage to this by threatening her life or even his own. "If you leave, I will find you and kill you," or "I can't live without you, and if you leave, I will kill myself" or "You may be able to hide from me, but I know where your parents live."

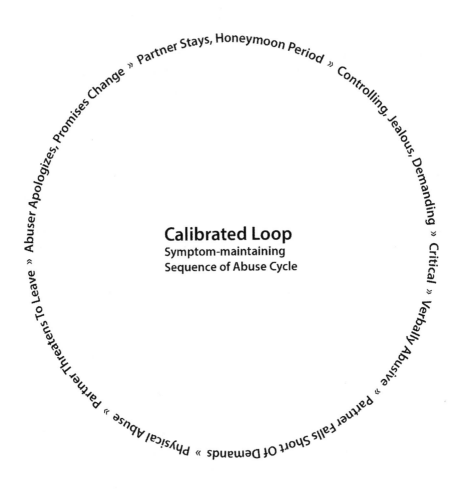

Calibrated Loop
Symptom-maintaining
Sequence of Abuse Cycle

Partner Stays, Honeymoon Period » Controlling, Jealous, Demanding » Critical » Verbally Abusive » Partner Falls Short Of Demands » Physical Abuse » Partner Threatens To Leave » Abuser Apologizes, Promises Change »

Combining Mindfulness and Cognitive Therapy as Recovery Tools

Life is a constant movement from pleasurable states to painful states. Pain in life is inevitable, but suffering is optional and pleasure does not last indefinitely. (Muesse, 2011)

Most, if not all, addicts use a chemical or process addiction to maintain pleasure and avoid pain. A large hurtle in recovery is learning to cope with everyday emotional, mental, and physical pain without resorting to a drug or a process. Making this more difficult is the buildup of economic, relationship, and career consequences accumulated during the period of time that the addict actively engaged in their addiction.

Let's start by examining the difference between pain and suffering. *Pain* is what we experience as a result of an injury, an illness, a weakness in our bodies, or as a result of a loss such as the death of a loved one. *Suffering* is what we do to exaggerate the pain by the way we perceive it, and what we tell ourselves about the pain.

Think about the pain associated with the loss of a meaningful relationship. Grief is a natural response to loss, and most would consider grief to be painful. We add suffering to that pain if we tell ourselves that the pain is unbearable or that this pain will never end.

Let's examine some beliefs in cognitive therapy that add to suffering. Cognitive therapy, or what was originally called Rational Emotive Therapy, was developed by Albert Ellis (Corey, 1996). Begin with the alphabet:

- **A is for activating events**. These are all the things that are continuously presented to our senses – the things we see, hear, smell, touch and taste.
- **B is our belief system** and it has two parts: how we perceive the activating event and what we tell ourselves about it.
- **C is for the consequences** that follow, which can be emotional or physical.

Consider these two different examples: You see a small spider running across your living room floor (activating event). You think to yourself, *That's irritating because I just had the exterminator here!* (belief system). You step on the spider.(consequence: a serious one for the spider)

Example 2: You see a spider running across your living room floor. (same activating event). However now, you perceive the spider as a threat to your life and tell yourself you are in serious danger (belief system). As a result of B, you are frightened, your heart begins to race you and you run from your house barefoot into the snow. (emotional and physical consequences).

You may be wondering why we call B a belief system and not just a thought. Typically, the way we perceive things and what we tell ourselves about them have been deeply engrained in our minds since childhood. In the case of a spider phobia, we may have even picked it up from watching one of our parents react to a spider. There are many different writers who have categorized beliefs that lead to suffering; Ellis originally developed what he called 12 irrational beliefs (Corey, 1996). We will identify six of those beliefs: Assumption, Awfulizing, Catastrophizing, Expectation, Evaluation, and Generalizing.

- **Assumption** is looking at the behavior or lack of behavior of another person and assuming the motivation or what they may be doing when you can't see them. Think about caring for a child whose behavior is less than perfect. We may think to ourselves, *They're doing that just to irritate me.* Or a spouse who assumes their partner is having an affair, simply because they are late arriving home from work. Both of these examples can lead to needless suffering.
- **Awfulizing** perceives an activating event and adds the belief, *this is awful and terrible and I can't stand it.*
- **Catastrophizing** is assuming a future event will happen and telling ourselves we won't be able to stand it.
- The key to **expectation** is the word should, often connected with right and wrong. *My candidate should win the election because he is morally superior to the other candidate.*

- **Evaluation** also has a moral component and usually involves judging ourselves or someone else as bad or stupid based on little or no evidence.
- Finally, **generalizing** is going from the specific to the general, for example, seeing a few crumbs on the counter and saying *There are crumbs all over this kitchen!*

Through these examples, you can see that the way you perceive an event and what you tell yourself about it greatly changes the consequences of that event.

This is where mindfulness comes in. Jon Kabat-Zinn (1990) defined mindfulness as awareness that arises though paying attention, on purpose, in the present moment, non-judgmentally. Mindfulness is the aware, balanced acceptance of the present experience. It refers to opening up to or receiving the present moment – pleasant or unpleasant – just as it is, without either clinging to it or rejecting it, according to Sylvia Boorstein. So the first step after learning the ABCs is to be aware of what you are doing. What is the activating event, what are you telling yourself and how is that affecting the consequence?

The next step is D, which is to **dispute** or question B. We can do this by asking ourselves various questions such as: Where is the evidence for Assumptions? What are the actual consequences for Awfulizing? If the worst does happen, what are the actual consequences for Catastrophizing. Why should I (or he or she) in regard to Expectation? Is that the sum total of me for Evaluation? What are the specifics for Generalizing? Hopefully these questions will help us look at what is actually occurring.

From there we can move to E, which Ellis referred to as **Effects**, but after disputing the Beliefs, there seems to be another step, because there is still an activating event that needs to be addressed, so let's consider some other possibilities for E.

One is to **Exchange** B with thoughts that keep our emotions more in line with the activating event. Many mistakenly believe that cognitive therapy is attempting to eliminate emotion, but its goal is only to eliminate the excesses of emotion, or, like mindfulness, to eliminate the suffering while recognizing the pain. For instance, we can Exchange the notion of Assumption with *I'll cross that bridge IF I come to it.*

With Catastrophizing, we can say to ourselves, *IF that happens, I won't like it, but I can live with it.* For Expectation, we can acknowledge that we are all fallible human beings who make mistakes and aren't perfect. For Evaluation, we can say *I am more than this particular behavior.* And for Generalizing, we can choose to look at only what is in front of us while staying in the moment.

We can also use E to **Escort** our thinking to a different event in the present. This is where it's always best to focus on our breathing, since our breathing is always in the present moment, and because it is something we can control. With anxiety, our breathing is often rapid and shallow, and we can change that to slow deep breaths.

We can also use E to **Examine** the consequences – both short and long term. If you walk by a bar on a hot summer day, the Activating event may be the smell of beer, which you have learned to associate with something pleasant. You tell yourself that a beer sure would taste good on a hot day. While that may be true, what are the long-term consequences? That beer may lead you to obsessing about another beer, and another, until you are back into a self-destructive pattern that you have visited too many times before.

Another advantage of mindfulness in recovery comes particularly for those addicts who have difficulty with the higher power concept. The first three steps in AA are admitting powerlessness over our drug or process of choice; admitting that our life has become unmanageable because of it; and recognizing that a higher power can restore us to sanity. This is often where people in the early phases of recovery have problems, because they only associate a higher power with God, when in reality, it can be anything. In fact, your higher power can simply be values. Some people will tell you that mindfulness comes originally from Buddha, but Buddhism does not require a belief in a god. This is evident in the Buddhist "commandments," which they call precepts, which are refraining from:

1. Harming living things
2. Taking what is not given
3. Sexual misconduct
4. Lying or gossip
5. Taking intoxicating substances

(Muesse, 2011)

Notice that these boil down to something similar to the Christian Ten Commandments, but with an absence of the first three that pertain to God. We can probably boil them down further to **honesty** and **love**, and since none of us are able to master these completely, they are definitely a power greater than ourselves. One might argue that the values of honesty and love can not only help addicts to recover, but can also restore the universe to sanity.

Homework:

1. Find a quiet place and get into a comfortable position, then simply concentrate on your breathing. If you are like most, after a very short time, your mind will begin to wander. When you become aware of this, simply escort your mind back to your breathing. Do this without judgment of yourself or others. Start by doing this for 15 minutes at a time.
2. Think back to a time when you found yourself getting more upset than the situation warranted. What was the activating event? How did you perceive it? What did you tell yourself about the event? What were the emotional and physical consequences? How can you dispute what you believed at B? With what could you exchange that belief? While you are thinking of that situation, concentrate on your breathing, and without judgment, try changing your breathing. Examine how the consequences would have changed had you applied mindfulness and cognitive approaches.

BIBLIOGRAPHY

Altman, Donald, "The Mindfulness Tool Box, Premier Publishing Media, 2014

Briere, John, "Reconsidering Trauma Treatment Advances, Relational Issues and Mindfulness in Integrated Trauma Therapy," Recorded Professional Seminar, Institute for the Advancement of Human Behavior

Corey, Gerald, "Theory and Practice of Counseling and Psychotherapy," Brooks/Cole Publishing Company, Fifth Addition, 1996

Kabat-Zinn, Jon, "Full Catastrophe Living: Using the Wisdom of Your Body and Mind to Face Stress, Pain and Illness," Delacorte Press, 1990

Kabat-Zinn, Jon, "Wherever You Go There You Are: Mindfulness Meditation in Everyday Life," Hyperion Books, 1997

Kabat-Zinn, Jon and Myla, "Everyday Blessings," Hyperion Books, 1998

Kabat-Zinn, Jon; Teasedale, John; Williams, Mark; Zindel Segal; "The Mindful Way Through Depression," Guilford Press, 2007

Kelly-Gangi, Carol, "Quotes For Mindfulness – Timeless Wisdom for the Modern World," Fall River Press, 2016

Muesse, Mark W., "Practicing Mindfulness: An Introduction to Meditation," The Great Courses, The Teaching Company, 2011

ANGER
By Kimberly Groll LCPC, CADC, CAMT

In the years I have been practicing, I have dealt with a lot of anger issues. As I sit down with my clients and go over their history, I have found that anger has been a part of their lives for many years. If a parent calls me about their child with wanting him or her to come in and see me to deal with their anger, I always ask the parent when did you first start seeing signs of anger being displayed? I am amazed when I am told by the parent that they have witnessed anger episodes for many years prior to this initial phone call. It is only now that their child is experiencing some sort of trouble with the law that they are now seeking treatment.

What I would like for parents to know is the longer you ignore signs or symptoms with anger the worse it can be for the child and those surrounded by the child. If you are noticing abnormal behavior stemming from anger, it needs to be addressed. I have seen too many situations that could be avoided if only the adolescent had early treatment to learn the necessary coping skills to move forward in a positive manner.

As we get older and continue with negative behaviors, these negative behaviors will continue to develop with time. In some cases the negative situations can start evolving into more troublesome behavior and by allowing these behaviors to continue can only do harm. The longer the behaviors continue, the harder they are to get under control. We all know that change gets more difficult with the growing years after we establish certain habits; therefore, it needs to be addressed and dealt with in the early stages so a person has a chance to learn new techniques and develop new learned patterns of behavior while putting forth the effort to make the changes.

Counseling Tips: When a person recognizes tense feelings and possible rage building, it is a sign to take a time out in one's thoughts and figure out what is going on within that individual. No one can make you angry; only you can make yourself angry. Take the time to figure out what is causing you to feel tense or angry at that moment. Is this due to unresolved issues or built up tension due to past actions caused by another individual in which you disagreed with but did nothing about it at that time? If you are not resolving issues that arise at the time they are occurring, perhaps you are stuffing all these negative feelings. When something happens in a current moment and you are really upset with previous issues, this is when you might begin to feel yourself getting angry. This is a time when you need to ask yourself what is really going on with me. Why am I so tense or angry and why is this bothering me? If you find your anger is due to pent up feelings from unresolved past issues, it would be a good idea to learn effective communication skills to learn how to deal with your issues in a constructive manner with getting your point across in a healthy manner. It is important to deal with the issues as they occur by addressing the situation and expressing your feelings with explaining what it is that is upsetting you.

Using "I Statements" when you are speaking is an effective way to communicate. An example of this would be "I feel you are not being fair." "I understand what you are saying; however, can you give me a chance to explain." "I would like it if we could just sit down and talk about this?" If you or the other person feels as if the anger is too out of control at that time to carry on with an easy going conversation, take a time out. Use this time to reflect on the issue and go for a walk or leave the room. The suggested time would be fifteen minutes. This is not always possible to do; however, address the issue as soon as you can and don't let days or weeks go by without addressing the issue. This can cause a bigger blow-up later on.

Newspaper Column Written on Anger

In this month's column, I would like to bring attention to anger. It appears there is a lot of anger in the air! I have been receiving calls, reading e-mails, and dealing with numerous court-mandated cases, all dealing with anger. I felt it important to bring this topic to the reader's attention. So, what is anger? "Anger is a strong feeling of displeasure and antagonism, or an automatic reaction to any real or imagined insult, frustration, or injustice, producing emotional agitation seeking expression."

We all have anger; it is a primary emotion and a signal that something is blocking one's wants, needs or goals. What a person needs to understand is anger is a response to something going on within the individual. This can be related to fear, helplessness, frustrated goals, embarrassment, tense or difficult situations, false beliefs, conflicts, or stress. How we handle our anger is up to the individual and there are healthy ways to learn to deal with anger.

The earlier you learn the skills to keep anger under control, the better chances a person will have with avoiding serious repercussions later in life. I have had many people say to me after entering my anger management sessions, "I wish I learned this when I was younger." Learning the necessary skills to keep your anger in control by turning the negative energy into positive energy can save a person from a lot of pent up anger, and acting out with that anger.

Oftentimes when anger is left unattended it can lead to the police being called, domestic violence, battery charges, felony charges, and even death. It is a costly venture when it gets into the court systems, and people are then mandated by the court to enter into anger management. From my experience, and from what I am seeing today with anger, I advise people who are experiencing any anger issues to take it seriously, and seek treatment early on if this is possible. To let it get out of control later in years can only bring unpleasant results for the individual and those surrounded by the anger.

With anger in the air, I bring you this month's letter:

Dear Counselor,

I don't know where to begin. I have been surrounded by anger my whole life. I remember my father being angry and always yelling and throwing things around when I was a child. Today, as I am raising a family of my own, I am starting to see this pattern with my son. It started with yelling, and eventually graduated to throwing things, cussing at me, and damaging our property. I walk on egg shells and I never know when something is going to upset him. I want to bring him into counseling, but I am afraid he won't go and then I fear he will get upset and I have to deal with his attitude. I don't know what to do and I am wondering if you have any suggestions?

Living with Fear,
S.C. (Aurora)

Dear S.C.,

I would consider therapy for anger management. If you are walking on egg shells and letting your son control your environment, it will only get worse, and his anger will continue to grow. His anger is from emotions he needs to learn to control and deal with in a healthy manner. The sooner he is able to learn this control, the better his chances will be at moving into adult life without the pent up anger and possible destruction to himself and others.

Learning how to cope with anger begins with learning about emotional intelligence. Emotional Intelligence deals with self-awareness, which is the capacity for understanding one's emotions. This leads into learning about self-management and the capacity for effectively managing one's motives and regulating behavior. It includes learning about self-motivation where emotions are monitored and controlled in order to achieve goals. Social awareness is a huge piece in the learning process of managing anger where empathy is the capacity for understanding what others are saying and feeling and why they feel and act as they do. Lastly there is relationship management and the capacity for acting in such a way that one is able to get desired results from others and reach personal goals.

There are many components that go into learning how to deal with one's anger. If you are witnessing any type of anger within your household, especially with younger individuals, you may want to get this under control before it gets out of control.

Sincerely,
Counselor Kimberly

Heroin and Painkillers

Heroin is now considered by many doctors, politicians, and journalists to be an epidemic. In a editorial in the *Chicago Tribune* on September 11 titled "Illinois vs. the Opioid Epidemic," the Tribune reported that 1,889 people in Illinois alone died from opioid overdoses last year. West Virginia ranks first in opioid overdose deaths, followed by New Hampshire, Ohio and Kentucky. Middletown, Ohio, a town of 49,000, had 30 opioid overdose-related deaths in one week, according to an Aug. 29 article in *Sports Illustrated*.

Death from drug overdoses now exceeds the number of deaths from auto accidents and gun homicides, and we know these are not mutually exclusive numbers. In that same Tribune article, one man reported crashing three cars in one week while high on fentanyl. And certainly, a number of shooting deaths are related to heroin trafficking and distribution disagreements.

One of the side stories in *A Rose by any Other Name* is about a young man named Todd, which is similar in some respects to Scott's story in *Autumn Snow*. Both are athletes who become drug addicted, but in Todd's story, we learn about a path to drug addiction that has become all too common. In *Sports Illustrated* (June 22,2015), an article called "Smack Epidemic" explores the stories of athletes who go down a similar path that Todd has taken, many of which lead to death.

Oftentimes, it starts with a sports injury. In many cases, that injury leads to surgery, or at a minimum, time off the field, court, mat, or pool. This can be devastating to the athlete who sits and watches from the sidelines as they see their hopes and dreams of stardom slipping away. All athletes want to play – even those who are less athletically gifted. In many cases, injuries can become a financial disaster for student athletes hoping to earn a college scholarship.

Then along comes the answer to their problems – pain pills. Now, not only can they continue to play, but they can also enjoy the high that comes along with the pills.

For this athlete, there are any number of different outcomes. One possibility is the pain medication allows the athlete to continue to play the sport they love, and after the problem is resolved, they stop using the drug and continue on with their life.

The vast majority of people who take pain pills never do heroin, but athletes who take pain pills are twice as likely to move on to heroin than are non-athletes (SI, 2015). And, according to the NIDA (2015), 8 of 10 heroin users start out by abusing pain pills.

Another possibility is that the athlete is met with further disappointment. Perhaps they no longer can play at the level they played at prior to the injury. Maybe the pain masks the injury too well, causing the athlete to aggravate the injury and send him back to the training room. This can lead to more time off, and the disappointment can lead to additional drug abuse.

There can also be the problem of the athlete missing the relaxed or euphoric feeling the painkiller gave him, and here is where heroin can enter the picture. A $5 bag of heroin is typically much less expensive than the painkillers – which can run as much as $30 per pill – and heroin provides a more intense high.

Fentanyl is one of the big reasons for the large increase in heroin overdoses. It's estimated to be as much as 100 times stronger than heroin but with a much higher concentration. In fact, if Fentanyl were sugar, as few as three granules could be fatal. It is often mixed with heroin, which leads to fatalities.

In the 90s, we worried about how addicting cocaine was. My fear with a drug like Fentanyl is that users won't live long enough to become addicted.

Bibliography

Reiter, Ben, "The Slugger and the Scout;" Sports Illustrated, May 2, 2017

Wertheim, L. Jon, Ken Rodriquez, "Smack Epidemic: How Painkillers are Turning Young Athletes into Heroin Addicts," Sports Illustrated, June 22, 2015

Websites

Death by Fentanyl
   http://interactive.fusion.net/death-by-fentanyl/intro.html

Editorials and Blogs

"Illinois vs. the Opioid Epidemic," Tribune Editorials, Chicago Tribune, September 11, 2017

Bellum, Sara, "The Connection Between Pain Medications and Heroin; Teen/Drugs and Health Blog, NDA for Teens

Printed in the United States
By Bookmasters